my begrudging scent
matches

my begrudging scent matches

AN MMF OMEGAVERSE ROMANCE

NAOMI PHILLIPS

Copyright © 2024 by Naomi Phillips

All rights reserved.

No part of this publication may be reproduced, distributed, or transmitted in any form or by any means, including photocopying, recording, or other electronic or mechanical methods, without the prior written permission of the publisher, except as permitted by U.S. copyright law.

The story, all names, characters, and incidents portrayed in this production are fictitious. No identification with actual persons (living or deceased), places, buildings, and products is intended or should be inferred.

Book Cover by QAmber

Illustrations by Anastasia Kurtuluş

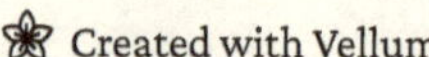 Created with Vellum

For all the people-pleasers. I will never judge you for all the exclamation points in your emails.

contents

quick guide to the omegaverse

If this is your first omegaverse romance, welcome! If it's not your first, welcome back. Here is some brief bookkeeping before we get started. Some defining of terms, if you will:

An **Omegaverse**, also known as A/B/O or Alpha/Beta/Omegaverse, is an alternate universe where all humans designate as either an Alpha, Beta, or Omega. None of the three designations are tied to gender, though genetics may play a part in which of the three someone designates as. Many omegaverses are tied to supernatural shifters, but this universe is not.

Alphas are, as the name denotes, usually the top of the hierarchical designation pyramid and as such are often in positions of power. An Alpha that is assigned male at birth has a **knot** at the base of their penis, which swells and expands during intercourse so that the Alpha can knot an Omega after climax. Female Alphas have an internal **lock** with the same ultimate purpose of locking the penis inside for a short amount of time (20 - 30 minutes) after climax.

By nature, Alphas want to take care of Omegas. They want to protect them and ensure that all of their needs are met. As such, they are usually more dominant in their relationships, but dynamics can vary from pack to pack.

Omegas are the physiological and biological matches to Alphas. They go through **heat cycles**, which are periods of intense hormonal spikes when Omegas rely on Alphas to take care of their physical needs. Heat cycles usually last for a few days, and in this time, Omegas experience physical distress, helped only by constant comfort and intense sexual stimulation.

During heat cycles, Omegas experience "nesting" instincts, and prefer to be in comfortable, secluded environments surrounded by safe and familiar scents, typically those of their pack mates. In this universe, heats happen quarterly for Omegas, and if they do not have an Alpha (or Alphas) to take care of them, they can go to a Heat Clinic where they'll be helped through their heats by employed Alphas. Because of their reliance on Alphas to help them through their heats, Omegas are often viewed as weak or vulnerable members of society.

Betas are basically normal humans that are otherwise unaffected by the hormonal cycles that rule the lives of Omegas and Alphas. Betas do not have a heightened sense of smell, nor unique genitals.

Alphas may choose to create a pack with other Alphas, Betas, and Omegas for a number of reasons, whether romantic entanglement, desire for shared power, or just because they like and trust one another. Omegas are usually mated to the pack's Alphas, completing a **mating bond**, which ties Alphas and Omegas to each other emotionally in a very permanent way. The mating bond is complete when an Alpha bites an Omega's neck or shoulder while knotting or locking.

Both Omegas and Alphas have a heightened sense of

smell, particularly for the scents of other Alphas and Omegas. A **Scent Match** is a soulmate—someone whose scent is more intoxicating than anyone else's. Scent Matches are very rare, and only exist between Alphas and Omegas.

And that should about cover it. Enjoy!

From: Alice Walton
To: Caleb Everett
Date: Monday, August 26, 2024 at 8:55 AM
Subject: Welcome to the team!

Dear Caleb!

My name is Alice Walton. I am the product marketing team lead here at Labyrinth Solutions. Logan just let me know that you'll be starting today as head of quality (congrats!) so I just wanted to say welcome! We will work together on a number of marketing deliverables from my team, so you'll be hearing more from me in the next few weeks.

I know you're remote for the next little while as you relocate, so please do reach out to me if you have any questions about the company, any of our software, or any of our procedures. We have really needed the right someone to fill your position, so I am thrilled that we have your expertise on the team. Looking forward to working with you!

All my best!
Alice Walton

————

From: Caleb Everett
To: Alice Walton
Date: Tuesday, August 27, 2024 at 3:22 PM
Subject: Re: Welcome to the team!

Alice,

Thanks for the note.

CE

————————

From: Alice Walton
To: Caleb Everett
Date: Monday, September 30, 2024 at 5:14 PM
Subject: Re: Press Release for Review

Howdy Caleb,

Just circling back on this request from last week. If you weren't able to look at that press release yet, go ahead and take it off your list. Grant sent notes over this morning and I just got it passed on to legal.

Scott is still awaiting feedback on his investor memo.

Thanks for all you do!

Alice

____

From: Caleb Everett
To: Alice Walton
Date: Monday, October 1, 2024 at 9:25 AM
Subject: Re: Re: Press Release for Review

Howdy,

Acknowledged.

CE

____

SLACK DM, OCTOBER 24TH, 2024

ALICE WALTON

Do you have 15 minutes to meet this week to go over the MRD? Maybe tomorrow?

CALEB EVERETT

Caleb: My calendar is up to date.

ALICE WALTON

Right. It just looked like it was fully blocked off until next Wednesday? MRDs are due Monday.

CALEB EVERETT

I'm aware. My calendar is up to date.

Send it over with your questions and I'll look at it today.

ALICE WALTON

Oookay. Thanks.

From: Caleb Everett
To: Alice Walton
Date: Monday, October 30, 2024 at 2:43 AM
Subject: December Release Plan

Alice,

Revisions attached.

CE

From: Alice Walton
To: Caleb Everett
Date: Monday, October 30, 2024 at 2:43 AM
Subject: Re: December Release Plan

Acknowledged.

AW

SLACK DM, NOVEMBER 7TH, 2024:

CALEB EVERETT

The photos on slides 7, 16, and 24 are outdated and distracting.

If you ask me.

ALICE WALTON

Well good thing I didn't :)

———————————

one

IN TRUE MANIC MONDAY FORM, Alice Walton's morning bus is late. Again.

She stands in her tennis shoes, one hand drafting an email on her phone, the other stuffed in her coat digging around for her bus pass. She *knows* she should keep it in her wallet so it doesn't get lost in the abyss that is her winter jacket's pockets, but she can only expect so much of her organization. She finds the pass as the bus pulls up—seven minutes late, mind you—stowed between three receipts, a tube of lip balm, and a hair tie. She fist-bumps the bus driver on the way in.

When she's finally squeezed into her seat beside the grumpy morning commuters, she sends off two emails and chimes in on the marketing team's group chat about a new investor report. Then there's the onslaught of texts from her mother.

MOM

I didn't mean to upset you.

I just meant that it might be good for you to spend the weeks between Thanksgiving and Christmas at home. Why have a flexible job if you never take advantage of it?

We just miss you, sweetheart!

Alice diligently tries not to let her eyes roll into her skull at that last one. She doesn't doubt that her family misses her, but she's under no guise that this is the only reason they want her to spend an extended period of time in her hometown.

MOM

And who knows what could happen? Lots of eligible Alphas here to help you through your first heat.

Ah, *bingo*. She doesn't even pretend like she's not trying to set Alice up with anywhere from one to three Alphas to mate with. Her mother has made her beliefs known regarding her youngest daughter's abysmal relationship status.

ALICE

There are Alphas in Boston, too.

Not that Alice seeks them out. Ever.

ALICE

Too busy to come home right now. Plus, I'm not going into heat anytime soon.

The last part is more of a manifestation than a truth.

Winter is only getting colder, but Alice feels constantly that she can't cool down. Every symptom is getting worse, the itchiness in her skin, the need . . . It's all a constant reminder of the inevitable.

She hates it.

ALICE

> I'll be home for a few days for Christmas, though!

While she waits to see if her assurances will be enough to dissuade her mom from pushing further on the subject, Alice jots out a response to her team's Slack message, but of course, her mom is just getting started:

MOM

> You just have so many wonderful qualities.

> Any Alpha would be so lucky to have you, they'd be fighting to court you if you gave them half the chance.

ALICE WALTON

> And what's my best quality, my empty womb?

As soon as Alice hits send on the message, she realizes that in switching back and forth between messengers, she's accidentally sent that to the work marketing chat.

"Shit shit shit," Alice quickly tries to unsend the message, but Scott sends a baby emoji and she knows the damage is already done. She deletes it anyway after smacking her palm against her forehead five times, much to the concern of the stranger squished in the seat next to hers.

ALICE WALTON

> Please disregard if you saw my previous message.

The bus' robotic voice intones the name of Alice's stop just as her phone lights up with an incoming call from her mother that she promptly declines. Three more texts from her mom fill the screen as she descends from the bus onto the sidewalk, all of which are about her daughter's heat, and how using the suppressants and deodorizers after age twenty-five is not only bad for her health, but a ticking time bomb that will lead to Alice going into heat in public where she's not safe.

She's heard this all before, even as recently as last month from her Omega doctor when she was getting her prescriptions refilled. The doctor was not discreet in handing Alice brochures to five different heat clinics in the city. They've been sitting crumpled in the bottom of Alice's purse ever since.

Alice would love to tell her mom that this is reasonably none of her business and that she has enough grandbabies already with how many Alice's older siblings have created, but she sighs and types something softer out instead.

ALICE

Headed into work. Love you, Mom. Tell dads I love them too.

Her mom means well, her whole family does. She recognizes that they all just want Alice to be happy. Her parents have been sickly, head-over-heels in love for almost four decades now. When all of their kids had been designated as Alphas or Omegas, they were thrilled that their children could experience the deep commitment, love, and comfort of a pack.

Her older siblings all got the memo. The two Omegas paired off before their twenty-second birthdays, the two Alphas a little later, now mated to 1-3 *someones,* and love to point out how woefully behind Alice is. It would be easier if she'd been designated as an Alpha. For an Alpha, twenty-six is a totally reasonable age to not still have a pack or an Omega. Nobody would bat an eye.

As the building elevator glides towards her floor, Alice repeats in her mind that her family means well—they really do, they are nice and kind and they *do mean well*—until she's mostly calm enough to face her coworkers.

Alice can't talk to any of her work friends about this since not a single one of them knows she's an Omega. Of the whole company, there's one happily mated Alpha on the executive team and two Omegas on the third floor who work in customer relations, but Alice keeps her distance from all of them.

Labyrinth Solutions is composed almost exclusively of Betas and she works hard to appear as one of them. Her mom would cry if she knew she'd been hiding her true self, but it's easier this way. That revelation would only bring more paperwork and gentle, knowing expressions than Alice cares to deal with.

That's the thing about being an Omega; it's novel, and everyone looks at you like you might go into heat at any moment. It would be mortifying enough to know that, by knowing she was an Omega, Mark from accounting would also be hyper-aware of her biology and would probably believe that she wants to have absolutely feral, ungodly sex with Alphas to create a minimum of 4.5 babies.

Horrifying.

On the list of attributes she wants her colleagues to know about her, *sexual needs* is not one of them.

Alice makes a pit stop in the bathroom to change into a shirt that she hasn't already sweated through and forces herself to face her reflection instead of avoiding it like the plague. Her concealer covers the smudges of gray under her eyes well enough and the flush on her cheeks could reasonably be from the cold.

Her neck is only going to keep getting hotter as the day goes on, though, so she pulls her frizzy red hair into a twist and clips it into place. She frees a few strands to frame her face in a way that she hopes looks intentionally messy instead of *messy messy*. Surveying herself in the mirror one last time, she nods. Despite how she feels, she *looks* fine, maybe even put together.

Healthy.

It will pass. The suppressants and her vibrator will hold out and she will be back to her average sweaty self in no time at all. These bouts are getting longer and more frequent, but they can't last forever. This is what she tells herself at least.

Alice psychs herself up a moment longer before pushing away from the counter, pulling her shoulders back, and heading into the office.

* * *

Alice has already eaten a granola bar and plans to skip lunch in favor of staying at her desk and downing two more when Lily, her closest friend and the senior graphic designer on her team, stops by her desk looking like she's going to explode with a secret.

"What happened?" Alice asks, her voice low.

"He's here," Lily says, as if Alice should know who she means. After a few more seconds of no reaction, Lily elaborates, "Caleb Everett."

Alice can't help but grimace at this news.

"Did you forget?"

"I tried to block out the idea of him coming to the office for as long as possible, so yes."

Lily laughs too loud at this, but nobody bats an eye as a tenant of Lily's personality is that she is *always* laughing too loud at things. Alice adores this about her. Lily is endearing and impossible to dislike, unlike Caleb fucking Everett, the bane of Alice's existence since he started at the company three months ago.

"Why couldn't he stay in Kansas?" Alice groans.

"Ohio."

"Same thing, basically. Middle America." Alice looks around, aware that she'd been so focused for hours that she hadn't noticed the general buzz of everyone. Someone *new*, the sweetheart of the Quality Assurance and Compliance Department.

Caleb's been working in his position for the last three months from Kansas—Ohio, whatever—until he could relocate closer to the Boston office. Everyone's excitement about him joining in person is undue. At least in Alice's opinion.

"They put him in the empty desk next to Scott," Lily reports. Alice scrunches her nose but can't help the way her head immediately turns in that direction. The desk is vacant, but she does see a new monitor on the tabletop next to one of the company water bottles. "I'm sure Logan will bring him by on his parade of introductions."

"I hope not," Alice grumbles, but when you speak of the Devil, he will appear, and sure enough, their boss rounds the corner with a tall, brown-haired man behind him. Alice recognizes him straight away from his email and LinkedIn photo; strong jaw, smooth hair, and teeth so nice they would scare a Victorian child. He's taller than she thought, only because she'd let herself imagine he was a small, frail man with a big ego.

And, wait. Is Caleb Everett... hot?

Alice squints at Caleb trying to find ways in which he's not aesthetically the ideal specimen of a man, only to look decidedly away when his eyes latch onto hers.

"Ah! There they are." Logan snaps his fingers—the man is always snapping, he's obsessed with snapping, it has to be his favorite thing. "Here, we have our illustrious Alice, and brilliant Lily."

"I wanted to be the brilliant one," Alice murmurs, and Lily's elbow thuds into her arm.

"So good to meet you in person," Lily shakes Caleb's hand like she's priming a pump. "Glad you finally came to your senses and moved to the city."

"I imagine it wasn't easy leaving all of those corn fields," Alice says. The full weight of Caleb's stare returns to her and Alice's breath hitches at the force of his undivided attention. She notes that his eyes are darker brown than fresh coffee, and also that her hands are now damp.

"Pumpkins," he corrects while offering his palm. Did his nostrils just flare? They did, Alice is certain. "My family grows pumpkins."

She recognizes his voice from months of Zoom calls but it's richer in person, solid. Alice wipes her palm on her pants as innocuously as she can manage with him staring at her all angry-bull-like, then brings her hand to meet his, only because everyone's watching and it would be rude not to. As soon as her skin touches his, though, she recognizes something about him. It's a primal recognition, one that makes her hair stand on end and neck flush.

He's an Alpha.

His hand lingers a moment too long as his own expression shows him trying to piece together *what* she is. He shouldn't be able to scent her, at least not with all of the scent blockers and deodorizers she's on.

Ideally, he will conclude she's a Beta with a suspicious biological pull toward him. Running into an Alpha in the workplace, rare as it may be, is exactly why she goes through the pain of hiding she's an Omega in the first place.

"A family of pumpkin farmers? Are you kidding? I love pumpkins!" Lily says. It breaks the moment between them and Alice pulls her hand away before letting it drop life-lessly at her side. Her skin tingles where it touched his.

"Definitely my favorite gourd," Alice looks away from Caleb's probing gaze. Anywhere else.

"Where's Grant?" Lily asks. "You didn't travel together?"

"We did," Caleb clears his throat.

"Grant got dragged into a training with legal," Logan chimes in. "Everyone wants a piece of the new guys."

Alice had almost forgotten about Grant moving to the office as well. The Thing 2 to Caleb's Thing 1. When Caleb was hired to manage the QA department, he was a package deal with the much friendlier legal and compliance expert Grant Jones.

They came from the same company and have added a load of value, both individually and together, since starting. If only Caleb could be as perfectly pleasant as his coun-terpart.

Lily has speculated that the two are boyfriends, but Alice isn't so sure about that idea. For one thing, Grant is nice and cool, and Caleb fucking sucks.

"How's that onboarding slide deck coming?" Logan asks Alice with his eyebrows waggling.

Alice shrugs. "Oh, you know. . . tedious. But just fine."

She deserves honor and accolades for not violently rolling her eyes when Logan pretends to look sympathetic —as if the slide deck wasn't one of *his* tasks he'd pawned off to her after procrastinating it for five weeks.

"Glad to hear it," Logan snaps his fingers again and grins, but Caleb doesn't. He's too busy looking at Alice like he knows her, or at least knows something about her. "We'll let you get back to it then."

Caleb doesn't say goodbye when they walk away, but the look he gives simmers on Alice's skin. With all the deodorizers and scent blockers she wears, there's no way he can tell she's an Omega. Still, he's noticed her. There's no avoiding him like she could if he was in another department; they collaborate weekly, if not daily.

Shit.

two

ALICE DOESN'T GET to meet Grant until the following morning when she shows up to work, twenty minutes early for once. She slides into the elevator just as it's about to close and doesn't recognize him at first. As a rule, she tries not to make eye contact in elevators in case the stranger on board wants to start a conversation that they won't have enough time to finish. Grueling.

"Alice?"

She looks up at the massive man who's built like a fucking linebacker for some reason, and recognizes the short dark hair, the mustache, the crooked smile. He's got a small gap between his teeth she hadn't noticed in their digital meetings. It might be the cutest thing she's ever seen.

"Grant! You are . . . so much taller than I thought you'd be."

"And you are just as tall as I thought you would be," he says.

"Really?"

"No, I thought you would be shorter. Your height is much more average than I expected." Alice grins at the admission. She's always liked Grant; he's sweet, sends emojis in his Slack messages, and always compliments her newsletters. He's a lot like a golden retriever if golden retrievers had sleek black hair, gray-blue eyes, and could probably squat two hundred and fifty pounds.

"I'm 5'8"," Alice says. "Some call that tall."

"Oh, I'm sure they do," Grant winks—honest to God, a wink before 9 AM. It disrupts Alice's breathing. "I'm glad to have run into you. You seem like just the person who can show me how to use the coffee contraption in the kitchen." Grant bumps his arm into hers as the elevator door slides open to their floor. She's still smiling up at him when she steps off and almost runs directly into Caleb Everett. Caleb's hand settles on her bicep to steady her.

Standing so close to him, Alice feels that recognition again, the connection on a cellular level drawing her to him as an Alpha. She knows better than to listen to that feeling, though, and steps backward.

"Good morning," Caleb says.

"Yeah. Morning," Alice mutters and readjusts her shoulder bag. Her shirt is damp and sticking to her stomach under her bra, thankfully covered by her puffy jacket. It doesn't matter what she wears, nothing feels like it lies on her skin right, especially with an Alpha standing in the small hallway.

"You two have met, then," Caleb says. Alice swears the look he's giving Grant is a meaningful one, like the men have a language gained from years of knowing each other. Maybe Lily was right about them being boyfriends after all.

"Yes, I was just hoping Alice here would show me how

to make a cup of coffee without ruining the fancy machine," Grant says, his face breaking from the secret conversation at hand to turn his charm back on Alice.

"Let me just put my stuff down. I'll meet you there in five?"

"Great," Grant veers off from Alice and, after a moment of hesitation, Caleb follows suit.

Other than the incident in the morning, Alice effectively avoids Caleb for the rest of the day. She's mostly stuck in meetings with various product teams which isn't ideal since she has three projects that need to be delivered before lunch tomorrow. This means another evening in the office.

Logan snaps his fingers and sings her praises as he leaves promptly at five, notably not offering help or an extension on any of the tasks he'd assigned to her. Lily tries to get Alice to call it, but eventually acquiesces and gives her a few snacks from her desk before leaving.

It's seven before Alice stands up again, a draft of what she's been working on sent to both Grant and Caleb for review first thing tomorrow if possible with a fervent peppering of *no worries if that deadline is too tight!* though she is totally worried.

Stretching her hands over her head, she looks around at the empty desks and the vacant private offices with their automatic lights long clicked off.

Her body isn't made for this. She's weary in her bones, even her spine is tired from pushing too far and on so many meds blocking her heat cycles. She needs to get home and shower then snuggle into a bundle of her favorite blankets with no concern if anyone will smell her perfuming for the rest of the night.

Her computer pings with a Slack message just as she's fantasizing about calling in sick to sleep in.

CALEB EVERETT

Just received your memo and report.

The screen shows that he is typing, then stops typing. No message comes through.

ALICE WALTON

Thanks. Please review it tomorrow morning if you can. Enjoy your night.

His reply is immediate.

CALEB EVERETT

Sure.

Are you still in the office?

Alice debates replying to the message when a third comes in.

CALEB EVERETT

Did Logan ask you to stay late? You shouldn't be there later than 5:30 if he's not.

ALICE WALTON

Just wrapping up. See you tomorrow.

Alice watches the chat, waiting for a response and wondering what the hell is wrong with him. Plenty of people work past five! Well, maybe not plenty, but probably *some*. Depending on the department. Either way, who is he, an overtime cop? She's salaried, so it's not like she'll get more money for her extra efforts.

Caleb starts and stops typing four different times before his account goes offline.

Alice heaves a sigh and shuts her laptop. She won't bring it home, it would be too tempting to do more work in the hopes of making tomorrow easier. No, she needs to rest, to sleep for as many hours as she possibly can, and somehow get through the rest of this week. The weekend is for locking herself inside and hibernating as long as she needs.

Alice rubs her eyes as she slides on her coat, mentally calculating how long until the next bus and if she has time to stop for a hotdog or not. *Probably not.* It'll be spicy noodles for dinner again, and if she has the energy, she'll add some vegetables and an egg.

It's nights like this when she sees the appeal of a relationship, a pack to help bear her burdens and make her dinner sometimes. Or even to just pick her up in their car. That way she doesn't have to fight to keep her eyes open on the humming, bumping bus with her head resting against the cold and fogging window.

Better yet, if she worked from home, she wouldn't have to brave public transport at all. Maybe then she wouldn't have a boss clapping and snapping and asking her to do his shit all the time. And if she *was* the boss, she wouldn't have to deal with one at all! She could only dream.

Alice brambles her way through the building and into the cold night air, heavy with unfallen snow. She daydreams about a blizzard so strong that nobody can leave their house and the wifi goes out. In this fantasy, she can burrow beneath a heated blanket with no possibility of an email or an unplanned Slack call pinging on her laptop.

She remembers days like this from her childhood when the weather was so bad that school was canceled and her family snuggled up together in the living room under a sea of blankets and pillows. The safety and warmth of the memory make her ache.

Standing beneath the bus stop, she wonders if Caleb has a pack at home, an Omega he takes care of. If they traveled here with him the same way Grant did. She jolts with what she should have thought of sooner: is Grant an Alpha, too? She hadn't spent long enough with him to even catch a whiff of his scent, and she hadn't gotten close enough to touch his skin, not even a handshake.

It's prudent that she spend as little time with them as possible. The further away she stays from them, the safer she will be. Her heat suppressants are barely working as is, she doesn't need to add the hormones of Alphas into the mix. The cocktail of suppressants, scent blockers, and deodorizers is an impermanent and, frankly, unsafe solution; the clock is rapidly ticking down to her inevitable first heat.

She needs to think about it, make a plan, and after that, a backup plan. She needs to figure out which one of those damn heat clinics she'll go to and probably schedule time off to make it happen—but not tonight. Tonight, she needs to get home, eat something, numb her brain, and snooze her alarm many times in the morning.

The bus pulls up, and as she mills on, her phone buzzes in her pocket. A work email.

From: Caleb Everett
To: Alice Walton
Date: Tuesday, November 12, 2024 at 7:32 PM

Subject: Re: Incentive Plan Notes
Alice,

Edits on your memo and incentive plan for tomorrow are attached. There aren't many.

Caleb

three

LILY SITS on the edge of Alice's desk just before lunch, so close that Alice must scoot away from her computer to see her friend's face.

Alice sniffs the air. There's something like the scent of a Christmas candle flooding her senses. "Are you wearing a new perfume? Why do you smell so good?"

"No?" Lily ducks her nose to her shoulder and sniffs. "If anything, I smell like I just ran a 5k. I just got out of that design meeting," Lily says, then lowers her voice. "Absolute hell."

"I thought that was this morning?" Alice asks and squints at her clock. It's noon.

"It was."

Alice grimaces. "What made the meeting need to be three hours long?"

"Two words: live designing."

Alice groans. She's all too familiar with having to make revisions on the fly in a conference room full of stakeholders. It's a unique kind of frustrating hell that often leaves drafts less cohesive than they started.

"Logan was being a nightmare," Lily whispers.

"His favorite thing to be."

"Caleb was great though, really sharp."

This information startles Alice, who has been diligently trying to forget that he exists and is in the same building as her. No wonder she hadn't seen him around this morning shooting her probing glances as he walked by or sending unapproachable Slack messages from his desk.

"Was he a jerk? Like, did he say anything rude?"

"I've literally never seen him be rude." Lily pulls open Alice's drawer and snags a bag of fruit snacks. "I still think you're seeing things, but who knows, maybe he saves it all for you."

The office is big, but not big enough that Caleb and Grant don't choose that time to walk by, each offering their polite hellos as they do.

Lily pushes off the desk. "Why are they both way hotter in person?"

Alice doesn't dignify that question with an answer. To herself, she had noticed that indeed they were both hotter than she expected. They're the *hottest-men-she's-ever-seen-in-real-life* kind of hot. This attraction is probably born from the fact that one or both of them are Alphas and not from true personal preference. She's not *really* attracted to either of them, she just thinks she is. It's not real. It's her biology tricking her into believing otherwise.

Lily walks back to her desk, leaving the lingering scent of the perfume or body lotion that Alice is determined to get from her later. She is about to dive back in on her project when a sea of email pings go off on the floor at once, not unlike an Amber Alert, but this one notifies that there are free sandwiches in the building lobby for their enjoyment.

Alice would guess that it's a celebration of Thing 1 and Thing 2 joining the corporate office, but the email doesn't mention that part. Logan's favoritism is clear, but he's not going to broadcast it after he got in trouble with HR the last time.

Based on the picture Logan's assistant shares of the cafeteria table, it's a shit ton of sandwiches, enough for everyone to eat two. Alice idly wonders if she'll be able to keep a couple hidden in the fridge for her to eat tonight when she will most likely have to stay until seven again.

As soon as she steps out of the stairwell ten minutes later, Alice is assaulted with the smell of toasted bread. Her dizziness at this is just another reminder that her heat suppressants are barely holding on. The deodorizers have been less effective, too, not lasting the whole eight hours on most days. She keeps smelling her scent on the bus ride home and can only pray that there are no Alphas on board.

Before Caleb and Grant got here, it didn't really matter if she perfumed at work because no Beta has a sense of smell strong enough to recognize it. As long as she steered clear of the Omegas on floor three, everyone would be none the wiser. Not like if she was in her hometown and every eligible Alpha in city limits would be knocking on her door trying to "protect her". . . Please, she knows what that means.

But now there's at least one, potentially two, Alphas on her floor to sniff around if she's not careful. The best way to be careful would be to stay the hell away from them at all costs.

Alice pastes a smile on her face and joins the party that's formed, decidedly not noticing Caleb and Grant immediately. If she *did* notice them, she'd see them laughing about something with Scott and Logan, and how all of their faces lit up with grins, making it impossible for her to get a soda from the drinks table behind them without seeing her.

Maybe she'd have Lily grab her one instead.

Alice reaches for the first two half subs she sees, one with roast beef, the other a turkey club, and makes sure to grab two of the little containers of sweet sandwich sauce for her to drench them in. She could drink this stuff, it's so good, an honest innovation.

She's about to make her break for the elevator to eat in peace at her desk when Logan calls out her name while, you guessed it, snapping his fingers. Logan is the single loudest man she's ever met, so there's no pretending she didn't hear him.

Alice turns to the group and nods, but it's obvious that they're waiting for her to come over to them. She takes a massive breath before joining their testosterone circle.

"Thanks for lunch," she says in greeting. "This is my favorite place."

"I can see that!" Logan jokes with a pointed look at her hands overflowing with her selections. "Great work on the incentives program proposal, it feels good to have that done ahead of schedule."

"Thanks," Alice says, then processes what he just said. Her brows draw together. "Wait, ahead of schedule, how? It was due today."

Logan purses his lips and looks towards the ceiling before nodding, "Right, I forgot to tell you. Turns out they don't need it until Friday."

In her periphery, Alice swears she sees Caleb tense up. She wants to scream at the news that Logan so conveniently forgot to tell her that the project *he* pawned off on her with a last-minute deadline actually wasn't as urgent as he said it was. Instead, she lets out a breathy little laugh, one too unhinged to sound genuine. Logan lacks any remorse or empathy; he knew she was staying late to finish his project that wasn't *actually* due today and he said nothing.

Alice pulls her lips into a closed-mouth smile. "*Cool.*"

She needs to get a grip on her frustration with her boss, and needs to keep her emotions in a steady place—make sure nothing sets her off. Logan says something to Scott and Grant, starting a conversation that effectively dismisses her.

She squeezes her free fist until her fingernails bite into her skin, distracting her barely. When she turns to finally acknowledge Caleb, he is staring at her with a startled look across his face. Not the composed, smiling, corporate dream boat he was just moments ago.

"Enjoy your sandwich," she says.

"Alice," Caleb says. *There's that voice again.* "Are you feeling well?"

Grant turns away from Scott and Logan after over-hearing the question, and his face now mirrors Caleb's concern. She squeezes her eyes shut for a second and nods.

"I just, um—I missed breakfast. I should go eat this before I pass out or something."

"Do you want a soda? Maybe some water?" Grant asks.

Are they always this helpful and worried? Her neck flames.

"Sparkling water, thanks. That's nice of you."

Grant grabs a chilled bottle from behind him, loosening the cap before handing it to her. The condensation drips over her fingers, it's soothing on her skin which is rivaling the temperature of the very sun at this point. She takes a sip and the fizz burns down her throat.

With the sandwiches in one hand, and the cold beverage in the other, Alice offers a smile before trying to extricate herself from the men so she can be alone somewhere cool, maybe the newly snowy roof or a corner in the ice locker that is the parking garage beneath the building. This is when someone puts a hand on her back in an attempt to squeeze past Alice for a soda.

"Excuse me," they say, but the touch still startles her. She practically jumps out of her skin, which makes her stumble. She finds herself pressed against Caleb's chest as he steadies her.

That's when she smells it. *Caleb's scent.*

It's what she smelled on Lily, the scent like a heater clicking on through dusty vents on Christmas morning. The pine tree in the living room with something sweet baking in the oven. It's comforting and warm, all the way to her spine. It tickles over her brain and zips through her, and... *Oh God, no, no, no.*

Alice sees when Caleb smells her scent too. His pupils blow wide. A puzzle piece has slid into place; there's a string that she wasn't aware of that's just pulled taught between them. It's so right. Her heart is fluttering, tumbling, soaring at the realization while her mind is firing alarms to take it back, right now, quickly, so they can forget immediately what they've just learned.

She should have never come down for sandwiches, no matter how hungry she was, because now she knows something she can't unknow.

She knows like the truth was cooked into her blood, the very materials of it making up her bones.

Caleb Everett isn't just an Alpha. He's her fucking *scent match.*

four

ALICE TOLD Lily she had to work the rest of the day remotely after lunch before fleeing the building like it was on fire. The Slack message came as soon as she got to the bus, wrapped sandwiches yet uneaten, but stuffed in her bag.

CALEB EVERETT

Can we talk?

Then another a few minutes later.

CALEB EVERETT

Where did you go?

Alice steadies herself for a moment, staring down at her cell phone before typing something out, deleting it twice, then finally hitting send.

ALICE WALTON

Was feeling sick. Working from home the rest of the day! Send an email if you need something.

There. That should send a clear enough message: she doesn't want to see him nor talk to him about whatever did, or did not, just transpire. Preferably ever again, but the rest of the day will have to do.

The ellipses indicating he's typing appear and disappear and Alice pretends not to be watching it like a hawk.

CALEB EVERETT

Can I see you? I can go to you.

There's something in her chest that tightens at the message, a giant fist squeezing her sternum, but she shakes herself and gulps down what's left of the sparkling water. She can't be humoring this, it's impossible. *They're* impossible. It would be in everyone's best interest to pretend it never happened.

Everything she's been doing: the suppressants, removing herself from her family, fighting every instinct, and staying away from all Alphas was to prevent *this*. Yes, she's an Omega, but why does that have to mean she's seen and treated differently than everyone else?

She doesn't know exactly what she wants yet. It's sure as hell not working at Labyrinth Solutions under Logan for the rest of her life, but she wants something different than what her mother had—being swept up into a pack so young and raising a million children.

She wants to take her time and fall in love slowly and not have her Omega hormones dictating everything she does or how everyone looks at her.

But, God, a scent match? Scent compatibility is one thing, but a true match is rare, the kind of thing someone doesn't expect to happen to them or any Omega or Alpha they know in their lifetime.

Alice runs her hands down her face and neck, which is

hotter than it should be. She wants to think maybe it's a fluke, but she can still smell him, his scent lingers on her skin like a curse.

"Shit." Alice switches to her calendar app and cancels her meetings for the rest of the day, trying not to breathe in the smell that is all around her, on her clothes, in her hair, on her tongue.

It's forty degrees outside, but as soon as she gets home, she turns off her heater and flings open every window, then lights four candles. Their conflicting artificial smells clash into something horrible, but it will do the trick. Or at least she hopes it will.

No shower is cold enough to cool what she's feeling, her body is buzzing—there's dread pooled in her chest. She stands under the icy spray anyway until her teeth are chattering. She tries not to think about dark brown eyes boring right into her and the smell of Christmas.

Wrapped in two towels, trying not to cry, Alice calls the only person who could possibly understand: her sister.

She answers on the second ring, all official, "This is Olivia."

Alice cries on the spot, her older sister's voice immediately comforting. "I think I met my scent match," she says, her voice wobbling.

"Give me five seconds." There's muttering through the line like Olivia is talking to someone with the phone pressed to her chest, then what sounds like a door clicking shut. "What did you just say?"

"I think I found my scent match." Alice's voice cracks at the last words.

"You think?"

"I know," Alice confirms. As much as she wishes otherwise, there's no way what she felt, what she knew without logic, wasn't real. "I scented this guy and I can't describe how I know other than I just. . ."

"Are you crying? Why are you crying?"

"Because I–I wasn't supposed to have one," Alice whines between little sobs. She's being dramatic, but she can't help it. It feels like the world is falling apart around her. "I didn't choose this. What if I wanted to be single forever?"

"Oh, Al," Olivia sighs. She's always shown sympathy and tentative support to Alice's choice to hide being an Omega—Olivia waited until she was twenty-seven before settling down with an Omega. But as an Alpha, Olivia had the privilege of not needing someone to help her through a heat. She wasn't a certifiable leach on the people around her, not like Alice who was certain she'd have to be. "You *never* want to be with someone? Won't you be lonely?"

"No, you're right, it's just that I—" Alice hiccups. "I'm not ready for a relationship. I sort of like my job, but I don't want to work there forever. I don't know *what* I want, or who, and it feels like the decisions are being taken from me! I'm not ready."

"You may never be fully ready," Olivia agrees, and it stings more than Alice would like to admit. "How could anyone be? Bonding with someone is incredibly permanent, nearly every part of your life changes. You'll never be fully prepared for all the ways that things will be different, but the point of having a pack is having someone, or multiple someones, who are there to navigate that with you. And mating with them is *your* choice. It can't just be one-sided."

Alice sniffles and remembers Olivia's bonding celebration, when she and her mate Johnathan beamed with love and excitement. They aren't scent matches, but they love each other fiercely. Their relationship is strong because they chose each other and keep choosing each other.

"But a scent match?" Olivia lets out a huge breath. "That's not something you can just ignore, Al."

Alice doesn't deny this while she tries to stop the influx of tears sliding down her cheeks, chin, and neck. Scent matches are the things of fairy tales. Of Alice's four siblings and parents, not one of them is bonded to a scent match.

"Have you told Mom?"

"No, are you kidding? *Please* do not tell Mom about this," Alice pleads. "I haven't told anyone. I wouldn't even let him talk to me. I just fled. Literally."

"You work with him? Please say it's not your boss."

"*No*, oh my God." Leave it to Olivia to show Alice the one silver lining: her scent match isn't Logan. "Not my boss. Just the guy who points out every week that I can't write something without misusing a comma."

"Him? What's his name again? Carter?"

"Caleb." There would be no way to permanently avoid him, not unless Alice quit her job and moved out of the city. But even then, he might still find a way to track her down.

Seems like the type.

"Does he want to be with you?" Olivia asks.

Alice hadn't considered the possibility that he didn't want to explore this, whatever *this* is. But of course, he could feel just as overwhelmed and out of control as she did. She'd always just assumed that all Alphas wanted to settle down if they had the opportunity. Unless he already has. . .

"I don't even know if he's single, Olivia, he could have a pack already!"

Homewrecker, homewrecker, homewrecker glides across the imaginary jumbotron in her brain, flashing red.

"Hey, hey, it's okay," Olivia soothes. "I know plenty of packs that have added members. It's rare, but I have a colleague with two Omegas in his."

The situation increases in potential mess and chaos the more Alice thinks about it. Committing to even one person feels like a leap, much less trying to join an already loving, committed pack when they didn't ask for her.

She's never even had a serious boyfriend, just a series of flings and hookups that ended with her being the weak link and getting out first before anyone could get too attached.

"What if I ignore it? It's not like we're bonded, it won't hurt me."

Olivia is quiet, which is usually a sign that she's trying to think through a reasonable way to say something Alice won't want to hear. Alice tenses in preparation.

"I can't speak to how you'd feel because I've never had a scent match. I don't know what that does to a person." There's a huge *but* coming, Alice can practically taste it. "But have you made a plan for your first heat yet?"

"What does my heat have to do with this?" Alice grumbles.

"Alice!"

"Liv, I know. I'm going to call a clinic. Work is just busy right now, I can't take a week off out of nowhere."

Alice drapes her damp towels on the rack and pulls on a loose night dress while she waits for her sister to chastise her, to tell her how reckless she's being. How she can't run away from her fate. Not for much longer, and certainly not forever.

Instead, Olivia lets out a long sigh through the line. "I think you should talk to him. Have a conversation. I'm not telling you to bond with the guy, just—what I think you need to do is open your heart a little bit."

Alice combs curl cream through her hair with her fingers and forces her gaze in the mirror to her face, taking in her puffy cheeks from crying and the dark undereye circles that never seem to lighten. Her skin is almost sallow, she thinks, sickly from the cocktail of medications and pushing herself too hard. But what other choice does she have?

"You've always been so independent, and I love that about you, it's a great thing," Olivia says. "But I'm afraid you'll regret not letting anyone in. Alone is no way to live."

The truth hits its mark and Alice, once again, has to breathe deep through her nose, or else the tears will start back up.

"Alice?"

"Yeah?"

"I love you," her sister says. Alice wipes away one rogue tear and nods, though Olivia can't see her.

"I love you too. Thanks for talking."

Alice hangs up first and shuts her phone off before she can see if any more messages came through on her Slack. It isn't even four yet, but she decides she's done for the day. She'll sleep for as many hours as she can and think about it again in the morning.

This is a problem for tomorrow.

five

AS MUCH AS she wants to stay home the next day, unfortunately, Alice can not avoid going in.

The department has a huge meeting to solidify plans for the first quarter and, as usual, she's put in charge. Despite having literal engineers and IT professionals one floor away, Logan acts like she is their only saving grace for setting up the technology.

Like, yes sure, she'll plan the meeting, keep everyone following the agenda, *and* set up the TV's in the boardroom again. It's not like there aren't interns and department assistants running around getting paid to figure that out.

Sure, sure.

When she gets in, she walks straight to her desk, not sparing a glance to where she knows both Caleb and Grant are already set up at their new cubicles. Now that she's scented Caleb, Alice can't get away from his scent lingering in every corner of this place. It makes her crave gingerbread and cinnamon rolls, and she keeps daydreaming about curling up in front of a fireplace on Christmas afternoon.

It's hard to believe that the rest of her coworkers can't smell him when it's a heady cologne that infects the air and makes her equal parts dizzy and comforted. The latter feeling is what concerns her.

As soon as she's sat with her laptop open, she receives two new messages in quick succession.

CALEB EVERETT

Good morning.

Can we talk?

Alice doesn't respond at first, taking her time to get out her planner, write down tasks on her list, and mark off a few from the day before. But she can't help but feel as though someone is watching her. When she looks across the office, sure enough, Caleb is standing, leaning against Grant's desk staring right at her. Grant is watching her, too, but he looks a lot less intense about it.

It's indecent, really. People in the office love to gossip, and anyone seeing Caleb look at her like she's his next meal is sure to make the rumor mill light the fuck up.

She watches him type something into his phone before her chat refreshes with another message.

CALEB EVERETT

please

Alice sighs and hovers her hands over the keyboard. No punctuation or capitalization? He's obviously in a bad way about this.

Caleb knows what she is—and what she is to him— and wants to talk about it. He probably wants to start bossing her around and introducing her to his family. Or maybe he wants to tell her that he's already happy in his current relationship and is definitely not looking to add an Omega into the mix.

Alice didn't dare tell anyone other than Olivia what had happened yesterday. Her mom would have flipped out and shown up with her three dads at her door with congratulatory balloons just waiting to meet their future son-in-law.

ALICE WALTON

About what?

CALEB EVERETT

You know what.

ALICE WALTON

My bandwidth isn't great today, but feel free to send any requests to my inbox and I can try to fit them in this week.

CALEB EVERETT

I can swing by your desk.

Alice's eyes widen at the threat and her fingers fly over her keyboard.

ALICE WALTON

Please, please do not.

If he came that close, she would fully scent him again, and from that alone, she would start perfuming her own horny Omega pheromones, enough to fill the whole floor. Caleb smelling this would probably result in *his* scent growing stronger and stronger, and nothing good could come from that cycle. Her dreams had been fitful, full of imagining exactly that. The imagining was against her will, she might add.

ALICE WALTON

I think that would be a very, very bad idea.

CALEB EVERETT

Alright, then when?

ALICE WALTON

I need to get through today. After the meeting. Please steer clear of me until then.

Caleb doesn't respond for a few minutes, and when she looks up at him, he is still looking at her—as if she's a puzzle he can't quite crack. Grant is watching, too, Alice can tell that he knows.

CALEB EVERETT

Fine.

Fine.

Even when talking with his scent match, he can't bring any liveliness to a message.

It was a long eight hours of avoiding getting any closer than a yard away from Caleb or Grant. Alice didn't think Grant was any harm, but with her suppressants hanging on by a thread, she didn't believe they'd do any good with another potential Alpha in the mix.

Staying away from Caleb doesn't mean that she's not currently as uncomfortable as she's ever been, though. Her clothes don't sit right on her body, the lights are too bright, giving her a blaring headache, and every perfume or cologne in the office that isn't Caleb's scent makes her nauseous. She wants to be home in her own bed, her nest, for all intents and purposes, with the blackout curtains drawn as she's buried beneath three blankets minimum.

The meeting was great, but Caleb being in person

meant that he could get under her skin in real-time. As they were wrapping up and defining action items, he kept taking things on her list and reassigning them to someone else in the room.

"Scott, you have bandwidth for that right?" or "Lisa, since you were in charge of that project for a similar client, would you take that over?" By the end of the meeting, Alice had three action items, about the same amount or more as everyone else, but it still felt wrong when the bulk share of the work was originally expected to be done by her.

Does Caleb think being an Omega makes her so incompetent? She can't humor the idea without her eye twitching.

After the day is technically done, she procrastinates at her desk by answering emails, squeezing her neon green stress ball, and otherwise doing things that could absolutely hold until Monday in the hopes that Caleb will just give up and leave.

But no, of course not.

At 5:30 on the dot, Caleb approaches her desk. He doesn't stand too close, but close enough that his scent greets her full force. She hates that this immediately helps lighten her headache.

"You got here early, you shouldn't stay late," he says. He's got a brown messenger bag slung over his shoulder and carries a red scarf on his arm. It looks soft, but Alice pointedly turns away from it before she can do something mortifying like asking if she can have it.

"Thanks for the concern, Mother." Alice is being short, trying to convince herself that part of her isn't thrilled about his worry for her. The traitorous part. None of her managers would tell her to work less, and in fact, they'd applaud her dedication and team spirit.

Caleb narrows his eyes on Alice, but she forces herself to look away from him as the blush creeps up her neck.

"I'm packing up." Alice kicks off her pumps and retrieves the boots she commutes in on really snowy days, stuffing her feet over the backs until her heels slip in.

"Did you walk here? I'll drive you home," he says.

"Bus," Alice says. "I prefer it."

Caleb looks as though every bit of him wants to insist she never take the bus again, but he holds his tongue. He must recognize that when it comes to Alice, they are already on rocky ground as it is.

Alice pulls on her coat, despite being on the verge of a heat flash the whole day. "Let's talk on the roof."

Again, if Caleb wants to object, he doesn't. He blindly follows behind Alice at a safe distance as they pass through the mostly empty floor and towards the stairs. They pass Grant who smiles warmly but doesn't follow.

"Are you and him a pack?" Alice asks once they've climbed a flight of stairs.

"Yes," Caleb says. "We've been together for a long time."

Alice doesn't know if he meant together as in just living together or together as in. . . *together*. . . Biblically, or whatever. It's not uncommon for two Alphas to be in a relationship, but rarely for long without an Omega joining the mix. Her own fathers shared romance through their whole unit, not only with her mother.

"What about you?" Caleb asks as Alice pushes open the door onto the roof. Cold air touches her face, and she relishes in it. "Do you have a pack?"

"No," she admits. "Lone wolf."

Caleb obviously is unable to hide just how startling this news is to him.

"How old are you?"

Alice walks to the wall, him following behind a step closer than she'd like. The concrete bricks are frigid beneath her palms as she looks out over the city. During this time of year, the sun is already half set by 5:30—it'll be mostly dark within the hour.

"I'm twenty-six," she says, ever aware of her spinster status. It's rare to meet an unmated Omega her age, and she's never met someone who's delayed their first heat as long as she has.

"Who helps you through your—"

"Nobody," Alice cuts him off before he can say the word *heat*. Just the fact that he's thinking about her in heat is doing strange things to her body. She takes a step further away from him. "And really, that is none of your business."

"Don't you think it is now? At least a little?" Caleb leans closer. She steps backward again until her lower back is pressed against the wall. She'll explode if she gets too close to him, she knows that she will. "You feel it, I know you do. You're my scent match."

"I don't see why you being my scent match means you now have a say in who helps me through my heat." Caleb huffs a laugh like she might be joking, but her expression tells him that she in fact couldn't be any more serious.

"I don't know where you grew up, but where I'm from, Alphas are supposed to be the ones to help their Omegas through their heats. Isn't that what you want? Instead of some sterile heat clinic? How can you not be happy about this?"

Alice tries not to scoff because Caleb truly has no idea. He's just like her parents and every other Alpha or Omega she's met, ushering her to settle down, to be happy to find an Alpha who will look after her so she doesn't have to work.

Like breeding is all she's good for when she has a lot more to offer. Plus, doesn't she deserve an Alpha who actually likes her? One who picks her for her finer qualities and not just how good she smells to them?

"I'm an Omega, Caleb, but that doesn't make me *your* Omega."

"The scent match indicates otherwise!" Caleb finally loses the cool composure he wears so well. Alice says nothing, just crosses her arms, and looks out at the city.

He will never understand what she feels, and she was stupid to even humor him being able to. How could he? A scent match is a life sentence to him, one he wouldn't dare try to fight.

Caleb takes a few breaths and looks out at the city, too. Lights inside of apartments and offices shine through windows as the sky turns a deep periwinkle.

"I'm just as surprised as you, but don't you think we should at least investigate this? I mean—just—you're my *scent match*." He says this like it's a wonder and a miracle, instead of the heady burden and affliction it feels like to Alice.

"I don't want that," Alice says. "I don't want to join a pack and be the perfect little Omega, I'm. . ." she trails off before she can admit how broken she feels when she compares herself to other Omegas. Like somehow when she was designated as an Omega, she wasn't bestowed any of the sweet, trusting, and demurring instincts she knows she should have, or something went wrong when she was born and she got all of the strong-willed stubbornness and none of the other traits that she was meant to have as an Omega.

"I don't want my scent to dictate the rest of my life. I want to choose my path, my people."

Alice finally peers at Caleb.

He really is exceptionally handsome. The downturn of his brows and his mouth, the slight curl to his hair at his neck. He looks calm enough, but the frantic searching way he looks at her belies his confusion and desperation. Alice understands the feeling; her entire body aches to move closer to him, to let him wrap her up.

"And please, you don't even *like* me, and now you want to take care of me through my first heat?" Alice laughs, but it's hollow.

"You haven't had your first heat?" Caleb asks.

"No, but again, not your business."

"And just what makes you think I don't like you?" Caleb demands after a moment of processing her assumption. "We just met on Monday."

"We did not just meet Monday," Alice spouts. "I've been working with you for months! You're constantly picking apart my work, or trying to get my tasks reassigned to someone else. It's pretty obvious what you think about me."

Caleb blinks at her words before shaking his head. "I'm the Quality Assurance Manager, Alice, it's literally my job to be meticulous about the work we send out," he reminds her. "Do you think I'm just marking up your work for fun? Christ, you should see the notes I send back to Scott!"

"Then why would you reassign my tasks to him?" They're both shouting now, loud enough that if anyone else was on the roof they would certainly be concerned. "I *know* that I can do a better job than him, and in half the time."

"Because you do triple the work of any male colleagues in your department on any given day. I can assure you that you are working harder than them. *Yes,* it's easier when you do the work, and *yes,* Scott needs two more iterations than you do, but you get paid the same, if not less, and do way more fucking work. It's not fair."

Alice's jaw hangs open for a moment, but she snaps it shut. She knows the work distribution is uneven, but she thought it was because she's the best. It's easier to just do the tasks than to go back and forth with others on the team who haven't picked up on it yet. And she didn't believe that this problem was something any of her male colleagues could even grasp, much less try to mitigate.

"You don't do yourself, or your team, any favors by doing everything," Caleb says. "You can only do everything alone for so long before you burn out."

She knows that they're talking about work, but she feels like the last remark was pointedly also *not* about work.

"But your emails. . ."

"Oh no, I've seen you *so sorry about that!* and *no worries if not!* matters that are definitely not your fault and are definitely worrisome if not—I email you like I do because I'm direct and I respect you."

"Well it makes you unpleasant and terse," Alice says. She's inched closer to him in her indignation.

"Well, I'd rather be unpleasant than an underpaid people-pleaser busting my ass for managers that don't see my value."

They're closer than she realized, less than a foot separating them on the cold rooftop, and in his frustration, Caleb is scenting unintentionally. The effect on Alice is immediate, filling every sense and gliding over her skin. It's like nothing she's ever experienced, being near her scent match like this. Her own scent starts to perfume out of her, mingling with his and making her lightheaded.

She staggers backwards from him, and Caleb brings his hand to her arm to steady her. The touch is like a live wire, even through her coat. She feels her slick between her legs just as he smells it.

Something ignites in his eyes, and without intending, a whine escapes from her throat.

"Get away from me," Alice snaps. Her stomach cramps hard, making her almost double over in pain. She hisses through her teeth at the sensation and Caleb takes a step toward her.

"You're going into heat," he says, alarmed.

"I know, just—I need you to get away from me. Please."

"Don't do this. You'll hurt yourself, just let me—"

"I can stop it," Alice lies through gritted teeth. It's wishful thinking more than anything. There's a clinic a few blocks away, she can make it there if she leaves right this moment, maybe. Hopefully.

It would have to do.

Alice clenches her fists until her fingernails dig into her soft palms. "I'll take care of it. Don't touch me."

Caleb looks pained, like he's going against his every instinct, but he backs away from her by a couple of steps.

"Please, d—don't follow me."

Alice retreats as quickly as her feet will let her, and heads for the roof's access door and down the first flight of stairs. She wrenches off her jacket first and foremost, then reaches into her bag to retrieve her water bottle. She chugs it with shaking hands, a few drops escaping and sliding down her chin and onto her neck.

She can feel her slick between her legs, the fire burning beneath her skin and behind her eyes. She's going into her first heat, and it's making her delirious. All she can think to do is go, get out, escape, and if she can't, then she wants to bury herself in a closet and hide. Scenting Caleb like that pushed her over the edge, her suppressants didn't even stand a chance.

Alice is down three flights when another whine escapes from her throat, this one louder than the last. She has to stop for a moment and grip the banister for dear life. There's wetness on her cheeks and she swipes at them realizing it's tears.

Above her, Alice hears a door slam open and she forces herself on. It didn't sound like the heavy metal creak of the roof door, but she can't be too careful. Her underwear is soaked, embarrassingly so, and she needs to get out, get home, or get to a clinic immediately.

Before she can make it down another flight, she hears a deep voice calling her name— it's Grant, she recognizes it, and he eats up the distance between them quickly. When his hand falls on Alice's bare forearm, her knees almost go out beneath her.

"Oh my God, Alice, are you—" He comes closer and his scent pulls another whimper from her chest. *Him too?* She thinks she might faint, his scent is so strong with hers, more woodsy than Caleb's, but nonetheless, it feels all the same. His eyes ignite, realizing it too.

Another. Fucking. Scent match.

"I'm going into heat," she confirms, panting. "I'm not supposed to be."

"I could smell it from my desk, why aren't you with your pack?"

"I don't *have* a pack," Alice barks, but another wave of his scent hits her and this time her knees really do go weak beneath her. Grant slides an arm around her waist and pulls her close to hold her upright.

"I can get to a clinic if I really—" Alice gasps because

this is when the pain starts in earnest. It's not light, or a gnawing ache, it's a sudden and intense bolt of agony directly in her abdomen that makes her whimper.

"How? On the fucking public bus? You won't make it," Grant says. Even in her distressed state, she knows that he's right.

She won't be able to walk to a clinic, even if it was right next door she wouldn't manage it. There is no stopping this, and she was delusional to think there was.

"My suppressants aren't working," she cries.

"You're still suppressing? How old are you—"

"Too old, I know, okay? This is my first heat, so if you're not going to shut the fuck up and knot me, then I need you to drive me to a clinic or get far, *far* away from me."

Grant's eyes rove over her face for a moment before he curses, then supports her weight as they move towards the door on the third floor.

"Go to the second," she says. "The developers are remote on Fridays."

Grant listens, pulling her down another two flights until they've reached the second floor. He swings the entry door open. Sure enough, it's completely quiet, the lights are off, and there's not a soul in sight. Not even a janitor is around to see them sneak into the bathroom and lock the door behind them.

"Tell me what you need," Grant says, as soon as they're inside, and another high, keening noise comes from Alice.

"I don't know, I don't know, I don't know," she whines, though she does know. She knows in a primal way that the only way she'll find relief right now is if he knots her, and fast. "My clothes—everything."

His hands descend onto her, pulling her shirt over her head, and then kneels as he slides her slacks down her legs, the cold air on her skin offering no relief. Grant stares wide-eyed at her mostly naked body for a moment. If she was any more in control of herself she might have felt self-conscious at the way his gaze travels across her curves.

"*Alice*," he says, and there's a strain to his voice that wasn't there before.

"It hurts, Grant. It hurts so much."

"Tell me what you need," he repeats, his voice now two octaves lower. "Say it."

He lifts beneath Alice's thighs and deposits her on the cold stone countertop. His face comes to her neck, his lips kissing and sucking at her burning skin, making her internal inferno rage even hotter. She bites down on her lower lip.

"Tell me what you need, Alice. Tell me it's okay that I take care of you."

"Your knot," She says. "Take care of me. Please."

As a reward, he pulls her soaked panties aside and presses one thick finger into her, met with no resistance. He curses again and Alice feels herself clench around him.

"God, you're good, aren't you?" he asks.

She wants to tell him that no, she is not good. She's a nightmare and the least eligible Omega in the great state of Massachusetts, perhaps the entire country. Instead, she whimpers as he adds another finger and begins to pump.

"More," she manages to say through the pain cinching around her stomach. "Grant, I need more."

"I'll give it to you," he says. " I'll take care of every little thing you need, you'll never need to want anything again."

No, no, no.

"Please," she doesn't deny his claim that he'll take care of her forever, she can't right now. Her ego was left on that rooftop when she went into heat in front of Caleb.

Grant halts the movement of his fingers and unzips his trousers before pulling free what might as well be the most beautiful thing she's ever seen. The only thing that will offer her any peace.

She's seen a hard dick with a knot before, even hooked up with a few Alphas back home, but the sight of it now, with her body raging and burning, feels like enough to set her aflame.

"Please what?" Grant strokes his shaft up and down, then grips his knot.

"*Please*, Grant."

"Try again." She searches his face, this one harder to say. She begs him with her eyes not to make her call him the one thing she's spent the last decade trying to avoid. "Alice. . ."

"Please, Alpha," she finally bites out. Grant's lips curl up into a smile. Not so golden retriever, after all, Grant is devious. He licks his fingers clean, something she never thought she would be *this* into before he notches the head of his cock at her entrance. Even the promise that he'll move makes her breath hitch, the precipice of pure relief.

"Again."

"Please, Alpha, please knot me."

His little smile turns to a full grin and in an instant he slides home. He pumps his cock into her, his knot bumping against her entrance with every thrust. Alice's pleas turn into a chant as he rocks into her, begging him to keep going, to go farther, to knot her, to help her feel better, *please, please, please, Alpha, please.*

Beneath the white light bulbs of the bathroom, Grant's knot breaches her entrance and expands, locking him in place as he begins to rut, grunting and murmuring right into her ear about how perfect she is, how she was made for him and Caleb, how he couldn't wait to give her every single thing and make her his world.

The niceties slide right off of her skin as she reaches the relief of a blissful climax, coming around his cock and squeezing his knot into an orgasm of his own. It makes her vision darken at the edges and her ears feel like she's underwater, but the pain in her abdomen and head lessens and she's not so frantic.

Alice is delirious as she comes down, Grant locked inside of her cradling her slightly shaking body against his, her naked chest to his clothed one. They're both panting and it feels like she finally can have a moment to breathe without catching fire.

Five minutes pass like this before Grant tenses, "Shit, you're on birth control right? Fuck, I couldn't even think—"

"Yes," Alice breathes. "IUD."

"I should've asked," Grant says. She's too out of sorts to assure him that the only thing he should've done was exactly what he did.

She knows it's not over, the relief will be short-lived. That intense feeling will be back soon, consuming her with pain and fever for as many days as it takes for her heat to break. This is why she doesn't fight Grant when he pulls back to look at her face and says he's going to take her home.

He pulls her head onto his chest and peppers some kisses against her sweaty hair then takes out his phone to make a call. She can just hear Caleb's surly voice through the line.

"Where is she?" He sounds crazed.

"The second floor bathroom. Get the car, we'll meet you downstairs in ten."

"On it."

The line beeps closed.

"It's your weekend," Alice murmurs and Grant just strokes his hand up and down her back. Between his touch and his scent, she's ready to fall asleep right here.

"Baby," Grant says. Alice forces open her heavy eyelids. She doesn't know how much longer has passed, but his knot has shrunken enough now that he's not stuck inside her. "I'm going to come out of you and then I'm going to help you get dressed, alright?"

She blinks a few times as she nods. Her body craves the connection and comfort of him, and a little whine escapes her mouth the moment he pulls out of her.

"I know baby," he soothes. He gets them both relatively cleaned up and her clothes back on her body, though every-thing feels horrendous against her skin.

"We'll be home soon and then you can get comfy."

Grant slides her bag onto his shoulder and takes her hand, so weak in his, before leading her out of the scent-filled bathroom, down the stairs, and into the cool parking garage. Caleb is already waiting for them and climbs out of the car to help as soon as the door opens.

His gaze doesn't leave Alice as he approaches.

"Oh, Alice," Caleb murmurs, a sweet and sorrowful empathy in his eyes.

Alice sniffles, and lifts one of her hands toward him, silently rescinding her command from the roof not to touch her. Caleb lets out a big breath and pulls her to his chest. His scent is mollifying. It soothes every stress racing through her skull. Her hands slide up his sides and grip the fabric of his shirt, admittedly relieved that he's here.

"We need to get her home," Grant says. He drops her bag and coat into the trunk, then opens the back door up. Caleb loads her into the back seat. She thinks Grant will join her there, but Caleb follows in after and pulls her back to his chest. For all of her protestation on the roof, his touch quiets the distressed parts of her. How could she have ever tried to deny him?

Caleb doesn't speak as they drive. He just holds Alice with his palm beneath her shirt, resting on her stomach, touching her searing skin. They don't even get to the freeway before she's asleep.

six

ALICE WAKES TO THAT FLAME, the scorch consuming her, and when she opens her eyes, they are there. Her clothes have been removed, which pleases her more than it startles her. Before she can even voice what she needs, their hands are on her.

Ever gently, Caleb lifts her back off of the bed so that Grant can settle behind her with his legs straddling either side of her hips. It puts him in the perfect place to whisper all of his Alpha platitudes into her ear. How they'll take care of her, how they know it burns, but they will make it better.

Meanwhile, Caleb stares between her legs like a man possessed.

"Do you want to taste her, Cay?" Grant asks. Caleb's eyes flick to his, then land on Alice's before looking back to her pussy. The thought of his mouth on her makes her writhe and spread her legs further.

"Can he taste you, Alice? Can he make you feel good before he makes the heat better?"

"Please," she says on a breath.

Caleb doesn't need to be asked twice. He goes to her

without grace, his lips and tongue immediately devouring her soaked cunt as he laps up the taste of her slick like it's his favorite treat.

"How does she taste?" Grant asks. When Caleb only grunts in reply, Grant pulls on his hair until both Caleb and Alice whimper at the lost contact.

"Share," Grant demands, which makes Caleb's eyes darken further. *Bossy.*

Alice doesn't imagine that, as an Alpha, Caleb likes to be told what to do while pleasuring her, but there's a hunger beneath his eyes that tells a different story. "Alice first."

Caleb looks at her, waiting for her permission, and when she nods, his mouth falls onto hers, crashing against her. God, the taste is absurd. Lewd and sweet—her own slick on his tongue mixing with his taste—it's making her insane. She grasps at him, pulling his hair to make him come closer and dig his tongue deeper into her mouth.

"Now me," Grant says, and Caleb's mouth is wrenched from Alice's to be put on Grant's. The two Alphas making out only sends her further into her frenzy, and she grinds against Caleb's thigh between her legs while she watches their mouths wrestle for dominance.

Another high-pitched noise escapes her and it pulls Caleb and Grant back to the matter at hand. Caleb kisses her once more, his tongue dipping into her mouth, before returning to her pussy.

"More, Caleb," she begs as his tongue probes into her.

"Sweetheart," Caleb groans before he sucks her clit into his mouth. It would usually take her longer, countless minutes to come from oral, but as soon as one of his fingers breaches her entrance, she's off and her orgasm moves through her, offering only the slightest relief.

It's euphoric and consuming, yet entirely not enough.

"More, I need—"

"We know, baby," Grant kisses down her neck and rolls her nipples between his fingers.

"Cay's going to give it to you."

"Is that what you want?" Caleb pulls away from her cunt after a final long lick and kneels between her open legs. "You want me to fill you up? Take that hurt away?"

"Alpha." She pulls Caleb's face down to hers and lets him kiss her senseless while two of his fingers now move in and out of her.

"You have to tell me, Alice, use your words."

He is *such* a dick.

She needs him immediately.

"Caleb, give me your knot," she says. "Alpha... please."

This breaks him, he has no cool nor control once she asks so nicely, calling him what he is. Caleb slides his cock home and at the feel of it, they both moan.

With Grant's chest pressed against Alice's back, Grant gives the pair his endless string of dirty words and encouragement asking them how it feels, if sinking into her is like coming home, if she likes to be fucked by her Alphas.

Grant reaches between Caleb and Alice, grabs Caleb's knot, and squeezes while Caleb pumps his shaft into her.

"Caleb's got a big knot, baby. Bigger than mine, it's going to make you so full."

"Christ," Caleb chokes out, his thrusts becoming more haphazard at Grant's pressure on his knot. Alice didn't know it would be like this, her Alphas touching each other, kissing, and sharing their affection—it's hot as fuck and her hips move on their own accord in an attempt to take Caleb deeper.

"Take our mate now, Caleb, show her how good it can feel to have you."

Grant moves his hands beneath Alice's knees where he pulls her open wider for Caleb. Caleb's knot slides into her and swells; the sensation becomes too much—she's too full, too sensitive, too hot. She couldn't hold herself back from coming even if she wanted to.

The orgasm ricochets through her, making her clamp down on Caleb's knot, taking everything he can give her until he's wrung out and slumped on top of her. She's high off of the sounds he's making, his grunts and groans, the way he's lost any ounce of his usual professional composure.

They're a pile of bodies, Alice sandwiched between them as they come down. The heat in her ebbs and their scents wash across the room and coat her senses. Theirs mix with hers, blending to make a heady, perfect scent. Something complete.

She drifts to sleep then. The pain in her abdomen abates. She's not in her home, but she knows that she's safe.

She's taken care of for now.

seven

ALICE DOESN'T KNOW how many days pass in her heat, only the delirium of it.

She is aware of her body, the pain that radiates through her insides tearing up her veins until one of her Alphas gives her relief. She can't stop crying if they aren't both there with her when she wakes, but the tears are short-lived.

She didn't speak much, but she knew that she begged them to complete the mating bond and make her theirs forever. Alice will be thankful later that they didn't give in to this request, considering she couldn't think straight, or could hardly think at all. Her days are spent sleeping and knotting and being fussed over by the warmest men she's ever known.

And then it breaks.

When her eyes blink open, Alice gains awareness of the room she's spent the last unknown number of days in. The scent of the three of them is heavy like a blanket. The room is cozy with substantial blackout curtains over the windows, and strands of dim yellow lights are hung on the walls. The sound of running water trails into the room through one of the doors.

Tucked beneath a heavy arm, she's barely covered by the soft linens on the bed. When she peers over her shoulder, she finds Caleb softly snoring. He's got the dark shadows of a beard, and his bare shoulder leads to a smooth torso she can't see the rest of.

There's a bright light coming from beneath the door, but after a few minutes, the light clicks off before the handle slowly turns, pushing the door open into the room. It's Grant wearing only a pair of sweatpants that hang low on his hips. His eyes go straight to Alice's. She stares back at him.

"Did it break?" he asks, his voice quiet enough to not wake Caleb.

She nods, and though her right mind has returned, her body hasn't gotten the memo. She feels like she might start sniffling if he doesn't start touching her again. She holds out a hand for him and he rushes across the room to take it, kneeling next to the bed to press soft, long kisses on her forehead, cheeks, and eyelids.

"Are you feeling okay?" Grant searches her face and uses one hand to hold her palm to his chest. There's a soft purring there.

"I feel weak, I think I need to shower, but I don't . . ." Alice's voice croaks, and her lips start to wobble against her best efforts.

"Oh, baby," Grant says, all sympathy, and presses another firm kiss to her temple. "I'm going to help you, okay?"

She's too tired to be embarrassed and just lets him guide her out of the bed and into the bathroom, leaving

Caleb to roll over and sleep a while longer. There's no doubt that he's exhausted from helping her through her heat.

Grant turns on the bathroom lights but dims them using a slider so they're about as low as the other room, then messes with the shower knobs until water starts spraying into the tub. Steam swims from around the curtain. He swipes his hand under it a few times before stripping out of his pants and bringing her, already naked, in with him.

Alice watches Grant clean her as confidently as everything else he does, with complete ease at the task at hand. He slathers soap around her body using his warm hands to wash her.

Her cheeks and neck are set aflame as he scrubs her breasts and between her legs, but she's not filled with the overwhelming need she remembers.

"How many days?" she asks as he massages shampoo into her scalp.

Grant hesitates, his fingers pausing their work. "Eight."

Alice turns around to face him, but a bit of shampoo drips into her eyes. She squeezes them shut while he rinses her hair clean. She'd never missed a full week of work, not in college, not since she started at the company, maybe not ever. And *eight days*? From what she knew, most heats only lasted four. Eight days of them taking care of her nonstop?

Their entire lives were overturned for Alice.

"I'm so sorry," she breathes.

"Stop that," Grant holds Alice's face between his hands and ducks his head to look into her eyes. "You have nothing to be sorry for. You're perfect."

She doesn't feel perfect, she feels like a heavy burden, a plague upon their house. But even with the running water washing their bodies clean, Alice can still smell Grant and herself—the perfect mingling of their scents.

Together they create something a little closer to whole.

His scent is different from Caleb's. Earthy and soothing, like vetiver and chamomile. She lets him pull her to his chest and they stand like that under the hot spray.

"You need to eat something," Grant says before turning off the shower. They stand quietly watching each other for a minute until goosebumps travel over Alice's arms.

The towels he bundles her in are some of the fluffiest she's ever felt. She lets him dry her limbs and wraps a towel around her hair. He retrieves a plush robe for her and she wants to wear it, but something is missing that she doesn't know how to ask for. She doesn't *want* to ask for it.

"What's the matter?" he asks.

"Can I, um," Alice sighs and probably looks as weak and defeated as she feels. "Can I have something with your scent? Caleb's too?"

"Of course." Grant retreats into the bedroom only to return a moment later with a soft, old tee shirt, a hoodie, and a pair of sweatpants. They do the trick, immediately offering comfort as soon as she puts them on, the scents of Caleb and Grant engulfing her own. "You don't have to be embarrassed to ask for what you need."

Alice keeps her eyes trained on the bathroom's tile countertop, but nods.

"Let's go downstairs. Caleb's cooking something."

When they walk through the room, the place where Caleb was is now empty and the bed has already been stripped of sheets. The comforter and other blankets sit in a pile on the carpet.

It smells like them. Heady like sex, too.

Though she's been here for eight days, she really sees

the house for the first time as they make their way towards the kitchen. It's new, or newly renovated, with smooth walls and bright wood floors. It's the middle of the night, something she couldn't tell with the blackout curtains, and as they shuffle down the stairs, the light of the moon filters in through large windows.

"Who's house is this? Yours or Caleb's?"

"Ours," Grant says and squeezes her hand once. "Caleb and I bought it together."

"Are you. . ."

"Together?" Grant peers over his shoulder and Alice shrugs. "We are."

They walk into the big kitchen where Caleb is shirtless and standing over the stove. The muscles of his back are defined and speckled with moles and freckles. Alice takes a seat on one of the bar stools, her body achy but warm bundled in their clothes.

Caleb and Grant being together doesn't surprise her after what she remembers of the first day of her heat; the intimacy that was shared between them with ease and confidence.

Maybe that means they're happy as they are. Just two Alphas that love each other and don't need an Omega to be complete. If anything, Alice was just a temporary thorn in their side before they could move back onto their life alone together. It would be better that way, scent matches or not —they must know that she's not pack Omega material. Too stubborn, too anxious, too much.

"Smells good," Grant says, squeezing Caleb's arm.

Grant fills up a glass with water and an electrolyte packet for Alice. She studies the two men as they move about each other. A hand placed on a back, a kiss dropped on a bare shoulder so natural like it's only one of a thousand moments just like it—there's an ease of movement as they glide through the kitchen, they're comfortable around each other.

"I'm going to get the bed made up," Grant says after setting the glass and a bowl of grapes in front of Alice.

Caleb stirs the liquid in the pot for a moment longer before he adds the lid and turns to look at Alice. "Nice hoodie," he says, a smirk pushing up his lip.

Is Caleb Everett *smirking*?

"Thank you," she says. What she really means is *thank you for everything, for eight days, for helping when the consequences of my decisions caught up to me*, but she knows she doesn't have to say so.

Caleb tilts his head and hesitates, really deliberating over something before maneuvering around the counter to pull her against his chest. She lets him.

Tomorrow she'll put a stop to all this. She'll tell them they don't have to pretend to want her with them just because she's an Omega and their scent matches—it won't hurt her feelings, really, it won't, and she's sure they can sort something out to work together without too much distraction.

Tonight, though, she lets Caleb curl his arms around her while she breathes in his scent.

Tonight, she lets them feed her and pet her hair and tuck her into the soft bed beneath fresh linens. And when she goes to sleep, she lets them hold her, one on either side of her, and imagines for just a moment that it can always be as simple and comfortable as this.

Tomorrow, she will leave, but tonight, she falls into the most peaceful sleep she's known in years.

eight

ALICE WAKES up in Grant and Caleb's empty bed, pale sunlight flits through the windows that were previously covered in dense curtains. She pushes up on one arm and rubs her eyes. Her bones are less heavy than they were last night—all of her usual aches are eased.

The suppressants and blockers took their toll on her body, just as everyone said they would, but she didn't know just how bad it had been until now. With her first heat done, she feels better than she has in months.

She's still in Caleb's hoodie, but at some point in the night, she kicked off the sweatpants . Their sheets are nicer than any of hers, the bed is so plush she could sink back into it for another heavy sleep, but something delicious smelling makes her stomach growl as if she's never eaten before.

"Fine," Alice mutters to herself. She swings her feet onto the plush carpet and flexes her toes before wiggling back into the baggy sweatpants. It's absurd to be embarrassed about her body around Caleb and Grant after they spent the last eight days doing things that she can hardly think about now without her face flaming, but the thought of them seeing her bare thighs this morning is horrifying.

Really, it would be best if she didn't have to see them at all. If she could sneak out without their notice and never speak of this again, that would be optimal. Unlikely, though, when she can hear them moving about downstairs.

There are a few unpacked boxes stacked in a corner. As she walks through the house, towards the smell and the noises coming from the kitchen, she sees various picture frames leaned against the walls, not yet hung up. They only moved in a few weeks ago and one of those weeks was taken up entirely by Alice, so of course their things are still half-packed.

When she pads into the kitchen, Caleb and Grant are both dressed, showered, shaved, and infinitely more put together than Alice is right now. Caleb pulls something out of the oven while Grant does the dishes, a picture of domestic bliss.

She realizes she's never seen either of them in anything but business clothes... or, well, naked. Grant wears corduroy pants and a sweatshirt, Caleb dark jeans and flannel; Alice hasn't looked in a mirror but she could make an educated guess that her red hair is a frizzy, snarled mess around her head.

She clears her throat and they both turn around as if an alarm just went off.

"You're up." Grant wipes his hands on a dish towel.

"How are you feeling?" Caleb removes his oven mitts and rounds the corner approaching her, but stops when she tenses. "What's wrong?"

Alice's mouth is dry, but she gulps.

"We didn't, um, bond, right?" she asks. She remembers

begging them to bite her, to seal the mating bond and take her, but doesn't remember if they did it.

"No," Grant says, his voice serious and low. "You'd feel it if we had. The connection."

Alice lets out a relieved huff.

Bonding would be horrifically permanent, something that could only be broken with a lot of pain, distance, and time. To Alice's mind, it was not a decision to be made with two strangers in the throes of a first heat. Many of Alice's siblings bonded during their first heat, but that was different. They wanted that, they'd had a conversation beforehand.

They hadn't gone into a sudden, frenzied heat at the place of their employment.

"Good," she says, then again, "good."

Caleb and Grant share a look that Alice catches but doesn't dwell on. Surely they're relieved too, right?

"Can I have some of that?" she points to the casserole. She has no clue what it is but it smells like cinnamon and blueberries and that tells her enough.

"Definitely, yeah—yes." Caleb grabs a bowl and cuts into what looks like oatmeal and steam billows up from the dish while Alice takes her place on the stool she sat on last night. "This is a blueberry oatmeal bake. You're not allergic, are you?"

Alice shakes her head and snatches the bowl, not letting it cool before taking a bite that promptly burns her tongue. It's delicious.

Grant pours a glass of orange juice and places it next to Alice, standing close enough that his scent fills her nose with the cinnamon of the breakfast.

"Thanks," Alice says. She blows on another spoonful. "I'll eat, then I'll get out of your hair."

Grant's eyebrows dip towards each other and he leans on the counter. "What do you mean out of our hair?"

Alice looks back and forth between them. They're both tense now, faces turned down in concern. With both of their attention on her, Alice feels warmth creeping back up her neck. They are exceptionally handsome.

"I've been in your house for nine days," she says around another bite. "You have your own lives to get back to, I'm sure."

"You're our scent match," Caleb says, picking right back up into their argument from the roof. "Both of us."

"Right," Alice says. "But I don't see why that has to. . . mean anything."

"Here we go," Grant mutters and puts his hands behind his head.

"You're not serious," Caleb insists. "You know how rare this is? Why would we not want anything to change?"

Alice takes her time chewing and drinking before answering. She doesn't know how to express this in a way that they can possibly understand. They're already a pack together, so it probably makes sense that they'd get an Omega—they'd want one eventually, and here she is, conveniently placed in their laps, single, and their scent matches to top it off.

"I'm not looking for a pack," she says finally. "Not that I thought you were implying I join—"

"We are," Grant cuts her off. "We want you in our pack, Alice."

"Well," Alice shrugs, searching for the right words. "I'm not—I don't want all that."

"All that," Caleb repeats, drawing out each word. He sounds like she's telling a joke he doesn't much appreciate. "Please do go on."

"It's not where I'm at," she says. "I can't be your doting, submissive, perfect little Omega that stays at home and raises your basketball team of little babies. It's not in my nature and I don't want it now, maybe not ever. I'm not ready."

"Why are we talking about *babies*? Caleb, did you mention babies?"

"I didn't," Caleb says.

"I'm not an idiot, I know what happens in a pack," Alice defends.

"I didn't say you were an idiot, but I am surprised that you think us wanting you to join our pack means that we want you barefoot and pregnant next month," Grant says. "We can take things slow, neither of us is trying to bond with you today—"

Caleb hums like he might in fact *love* to complete the mating bond today. Grant shoots daggers his way.

"We just want to explore this. How many people do you know that have the chance to get to know their scent match, Alice?" Grant finishes.

For her, the answer is zero, like she's sure it is for them. Rationally, she knows she should feel lucky to even have one scent match, much less *two* scent matches, and for them to not already be mated. But that's just it! Do Caleb and Grant only want to explore this *because* she's their scent match? Would they ever have come to her by their own interest?

Alice feels a cocktail of dread and fear and longing to be close to them while convincing herself that it's not *real* and she should stay away.

"I just . . . need some time," she says.

Neither of them look happy about it, but they agree. It's not like she can avoid them really, they work in an office together after all. Even if she did want to quit, she needs a job if she wants to keep living here, and her job is a good one for the most part.

She just needs some time to figure out what the hell to do about the two Alphas who want her forever.

* * *

When she goes into work on Monday morning, Alice tries to pretend that everything is normal. The story is that the three of them all came down with a horrific flu that knocked them on their asses for the entire week, and it works. When Grant speaks, people believe him. He has that sweetness about him. Everyone is sympathetic and none are suspicious.

Well, everyone other than Lily who has sent half a dozen texts peppering Alice with questions about how she and their hot coworkers managed to get the same sickness at the same time.

Once Lily was finally convinced that Alice wasn't involved in their week away, Lily started speculating about their personal lives.

LILY

Do you think they have a pack? Maybe their Omega was in heat? I get the feeling they're Alphas.

ALICE

Gah, gross. I try not to think about my colleagues as sexual beings.

Of course, she wants to tell her friend the truth. If anyone would be understanding, it's Lily. But she would have lots of questions and Alice is still not ready to think too deeply about these things herself. Lily's messages are tame compared to the barrage of texts from every single one of Alice's family members.

Apparently after day three, Caleb and Grant turned on Alice's phone only to find a voicemail inbox completely full, and dozens of texts ranging in levels of stress and concern. Grant had the honor of answering the phone when Alice's mother called for the fortieth time and broke the news that although Alice was in her first heat, she was being well looked after.

Her mom was beyond thrilled at the news and apparently had sent out a group message about the baby of the family finally going through her first heat and being taken care of by two of the sweetest Alphas. Alice was horrified by this, but unsurprised.

When Alice clicked on her phone after Caleb dropped her off yesterday, she was met with a slew of congratulations, questions, and otherwise nosiness from her family. She sent a message in the family group chat that she was alive and well and was way too tired to respond to any of their messages. She then powered down her phone and tried to get her head on straight for the next day.

It was a fitful night's sleep compared to the previous, but her body still feels so much better than it has, now free of the heat blockers she'd been taking since she turned twenty-one. Unfortunately, though, there's no escaping Grant and Caleb's scents.

They permeate the air she breathes and seep into her clothes. It's a shock to her that nobody else in the office can smell them. She can barely get any work done, too distracted trying *not* to be distracted by the Alphas twenty feet away.

Luckily, Thanksgiving is this week which means she

only has two more full days in the office to deal with them before the four-day weekend. That's when she'll do her best to forget about Caleb and Grant and the way her body perks up at the very thought of them touching her.

"Alice?" A dark voice interrupts her staring blankly at her computer screen. *Caleb.*

He stares at her like he might be able to tunnel into her thoughts if he looks hard enough. Her legs clench together under her desk because her body is traitorous and cruel. At least she's not dripping slick like she was last week. Her heat managed to make her *marginally* less horny all the time.

"Hm?"

Caleb's eyes rove over her desk, papers, notebooks, and sticky notes are scattered everywhere except for the section where she keeps all of the little trinkets and toys her nieces and nephews have given her. Plus, the few tiny horse figures that she bought herself.

She's suddenly self-conscious of them with Caleb looking at them like he is. Does he think they're childish? Is he judging the mess?

"You missed lunch," Caleb finally says. "It's 2:30."

"Observant," she says wryly and stands up to stretch her back. "I had a protein bar." Or at least she thinks she did. She peers into the trash can, sees a wrapper, and nods in confirmation. It was one of the expensive peanut butter chocolate ones they always keep stocked in the break room.

Alice catches his eyes lingering on her neck.

"Did you bring lunch?" Caleb asks. He's talking low enough that none of the nearby cubicles can hear, but Alice is still embarrassed by his attention.

Alice's eyes twitch with the effort not to roll them. "Another thing that is none of your business."

His face reflects hurt and, *great*, now Alice feels bad. She sighs and tilts her head.

"I brought leftover takeout," she says. "Thanks for the concern."

"Come to dinner with us tonight," he says, almost a whisper. "Please."

Alice looks away from Caleb only to see Lily watching them with rapt attention, her eyebrows waggling at Alice like they're an afternoon soap opera.

Alice pastes on her most professional smile.

"Not tonight," she says.

"Tomorrow then," Caleb says. "We'll cook, or we can go somewhere, whatever you want."

Whatever she wants.

That is a loaded concept as Alice currently has two wolves warring inside of her; there's her rational self that knows spending time with them will lead to confused feelings and then there's the horny ass Omega who wants nothing more than for Caleb and Grant to claim her in short order. Preferably now, in the office if needed.

"Why?" she asks. "You don't owe me anything. You've done more than enough."

"We want to be with you," Caleb says. "To spend time with you. Outside of board rooms."

Was this Grant's idea? She could see Grant wanting to spend time with her; he is kind and generally excited to interact with her in any way that he can. Caleb, on the other hand, is always either scowling in the distance or looking at Alice as if he's a lost puppy with no in-between.

"You don't even really know me," Alice says. Caleb's face breaks, and it's good that his back is now to Lily because she would be all over this, asking what Alice did to make him look so devastated.

"I want to know you better. We both do."

She clears her throat. "I don't think that's a good idea right now."

She can't trust that she'll make the most sound decisions, especially not if Caleb is going to be watching her like this and Grant too, both of them with their broad chests and thick fingers—oh absolutely not.

"Thank you, though." Alice grabs her empty water bottle and inches past him. "I'm going to have that lunch now."

"Right," Caleb says. His Adam's apple bobs, but Alice decidedly looks away from it and escapes to the kitchen where she tries to cool off and not think about anything. Especially not about *them*.

nine

BY 6 PM ON WEDNESDAY, the office has cleared out for the holiday and Alice has effectively dodged any meaningful conversations with Grant and Caleb despite their best efforts.

If it wasn't Grant stopping by her desk for a chat, it was Caleb leaving a donut and a note, or ordering her Thai food to be delivered promptly at 12:30 so she can't try and skip out on lunch. They were as focused and relentless in giving her attention as they were in their work. She had to respect that, even if it did make her stomach turn.

They were unmistakably courting her.

She'd watched her siblings court their mates, and vice versa. She would hear about it from friends, and reasonably knew it was a thing that would one day happen to her, but the abstract was much less stressful than it actually happening.

She worried that her heat, the courting, all of it, would make Caleb and Grant want to baby her—that by being an Omega, she'd need to receive softer feedback—but even with the extra attention to her eating habits, work has gone on as usual.

When Grant and Caleb collaborate on a document with Alice, they are as professional and thorough in their feedback as before—Caleb's messages aren't different in tone or style, and he still adds or removes no less than five commas from everything she sends him, though she sees his notes in a new light. He's not talking down to her or dismissing her requests, he's always been prompt and straightforward.

Alice has been trained to think that in order to excel in the workforce, she needs to be cheerful and effusive constantly to avoid coming off as a bitch. But maybe she can be more like Caleb.

Alice has been trying to emulate some of that energy in her correspondence, but earlier today when Logan asked her to send over some deliverables to their Canadian client before the end of the day, she still responded "Sure!" and ended up being the last person in the office because of it.

With all of her necessary emails sent, she crosses the task off of her agenda and starts packing everything up into her bag. Her eyes burn from all the screen time, she has to close them for a few breaths before standing up. It doesn't help that her sleep hasn't improved, she's still tossing and turning and is totally restless when she closes her eyes at night.

Exhaustion has started to show on her face again in a way that no makeup can *really* cover. Last night, she finally gave in and put on Grant's hoodie that she took, but even that only offered temporary comfort.

It's fine though. Everything is fine.

Alice is alive and well, and not liable to go into heat any time soon, at least not for another three months or so. That is more than enough time to potentially get over these pesky, persistent, and unwanted feelings she gets every time she sees Grant and Caleb talking, or when they catch her looking and they grin like it's already Christmas.

Alice sets her shoulders, raises her neck, and vows not to think about them for the rest of the evening. This plan goes immediately to shit, though, because when she pushes into the hallway from the office, Grant is there, almost panting with the tip of his nose red.

"Grant," she says and attempts a polite smile. Her scent is by no means subtle now that she's wearing fewer scent deodorizers. The blue of his eyes is eaten up momentarily by his expanding pupils.

He's not wearing his work bag, only a winter coat and a red scarf, which she recognizes as Caleb's. *Of course they share clothes.*

"Alice," he says, taking a step closer. "It's snowing."

"I saw," she says and looks down the hall to the floor length window. "I like the snow. It's peaceful."

"I was driving home and it kept snowing harder. I was thinking about you here working still, and, uh, I came back."

"Oh." Alice stands up straighter. "Why?"

Grant's eyes are fastidiously set on her lips, his own parted.

"I wanted to make sure you got home safe," he says. "Let me drive you."

Inexplicably, she takes a step closer. There's that string between them tugging her chest towards his, and she can't fight it. Not when she hasn't slept much in three days and especially not when he smells so perfect, like sweet chamomile calming her senses.

"I can take the bus," she says, a bit breathless at their sudden proximity.

"Don't be difficult," he says. It's a plea more than a command. Still, she inches closer, and so does he—they're less than a foot apart now. She smells him, and Caleb, too, lingering on Grant's clothes.

"I'm not difficult."

"You're a brat."

"And you're bossy," she quips, but her neck is tilted back so she can look at him in those scorching blue eyes, bright like the base of a flame.

"Christ," Grant breathes and before she knows it, his lips are against hers. She falls right into it, her bag slipping off of her shoulder before he scoops her against him. He doesn't kiss so much as he devours, his tongue sliding into her mouth for her to suck on and push against.

A tiny groan escapes him as she bites his lower lip, and his arms wrap even tighter around her.

There's this fire building in her chest, smoke tingles beneath her skin and through her veins. She's afraid she might combust just from this, just kissing him in a stale hallway beneath buzzing fluorescent lights. The only other sounds are the heater flowing through the vents and their frantic breaths.

Alice gathers a sparse grip on reality and pulls her face away from Grant's. He searches her face, none of the rakish confidence she saw last week. Only need, and desperation. He's gripping onto her for dear life. Their heavy breaths mingle together and the heat of his skin under her palm all feels right, but there's that niggling and persistent concern again.

"I have to go home," she says instead of spilling the secret fears bubbling inside of her. "I'm not feeling well."

"Let me take you," he says.

She gulps before giving a nod. She will let him because

he and Caleb have a nice car with heated seats and XM radio that will get her home faster than the bus, which is already slow even on a day with perfect weather. She will let him because she can only deny her body so much and walking away from him now would be too big an ask.

They untangle themselves from one another and walk to the elevator without touching. Once the doors slide shut, there's a brief, tense moment before Grant kisses her again. It's intense and messy, he kisses her so hard that her knees falter and she has to lean on the rail for support. He pulls back from her after only a minute of this, fixing his jacket just as the doors open to the parking garage.

Grant winds the scarf around Alice's neck twice, and it smells as much like Caleb as she hoped it would. The car is much the same, an envelope of their scents encasing her as soon as Grant closes the door behind her.

"Will Caleb be upset?" Alice asks once they've pulled out of the parking garage. "About, um, the kissing?"

"Why would he be upset?"

Alice chews on the inside of her lower lip. "Because you're together."

"We are." Grant nods. "I think if I was kissing anyone else he might be, and with good reason, but you're not just anyone. You're our missing piece."

Grant's candor about this makes Alice's cheeks burn. They're entering into dangerous territory, talking like this.

"You two seem happy enough."

"We are," Grant agrees. "I love him, and he loves me. We have a home together, a life we've built, it's all very neat, but we were always open to finding an Omega."

"Then why haven't you?" They are the most eligible Alphas Alice has ever met. They're hot, nice, and hard-working—Grant has a damn law degree and Caleb an MBA.

Undeniably, they're sexy, educated men, and Alice is to believe they haven't had their pick of Omegas before now? That *she* was the one to finally turn their heads?

"It wasn't right," Grant says, like it's the simplest thing in the world. Like the difference now is that she *is* right. "Caleb's been. . . yearning these last couple of years. I think he's been quietly hoping we'd find someone that fits with us for a long time."

"Does that make you feel bad?" Alice's mind rolls over the possibility that sweet, lovely Grant could be the one who hasn't really wanted this match, not Caleb.

"No," Grant smiles and a dimple shows on his cheek. Alice stuffs her hands under her legs to refrain from reaching out to touch it. "Caleb likes to take care of people. He's got a lot of love under that rigid exterior."

"Where is Caleb now?" She asks instead of digging further into this *missing piece* business.

"I dropped him at home. He has food to prep for tomorrow."

"Oh. Right." Tomorrow. Thanksgiving. It's usually one of her favorite holidays, but this year she will be spending it alone.

In trying to deflect her mom's probing questions, she hadn't booked her flight early enough. Now they're all too expensive, so she lied and told her parents she would be spending the day with one of her coworkers and vowed to spend at least a week back at home for Christmas. It's for the best, ultimately, because Alice doesn't know that she can deal with her family right now.

She'd assured her mother enough that she was safe, her heat was painless and, no, she didn't bond with either of the Alphas, but *Mom, lots of people wait nowadays, it's not a big deal.* Olivia is the only one who knows Caleb and

Grant are her scent matches, a secret Alice only prays her sister won't spill over turkey and mashed potatoes tomorrow.

"Do you have family in town?" Grant asks.

"None here," she admits.

"Do you miss them?" Grant asks. His eyes don't leave the icy road they're on, and it gives Alice the chance to really look at him. His straight nose and sharp jaw were now covered in a shadow.

"I do. They're a lot, but it's just because they care very deeply. I know I'm lucky to have them."

"Your mom sounded nice." Grant chuckles and part of Alice dies remembering that he talked to her mom while Alice was in heat in the same house. "She loves you."

"I'm sure she loves you, too, now," Alice says. "Forever indebted for helping her baby, blah, blah, I'm sure you heard all of that from her."

"I did," Grant admits. Alice can't help the smile that digs into her cheek.

"Is your family here? Is that why you took the job?"

"My parents are here. Caleb's got a pretty big family, but most of them are still in Ohio."

"The pumpkin farmers," she recalls.

"Exactly." Grant stops at a light and fiddles with the knobs before warm air blows through the vents. He turns on Alice's seat warmer, too, and she sinks further into the comfort and coziness of the space. "His parents flew in for the holiday, so it'll be quite the gathering tomorrow."

"Sounds like it."

After a few moments of silence, Grant lets out a big breath. "Please join us."

She doesn't know if he means join their pack or join them for dinner, but neither sounds like a safe option in her mission of not letting herself get any more attached than her body and biology would so like her to be.

"There'll be so much food, plenty of space—I know that everyone would love to meet you—"

"Meet me in what capacity?" She can't help but ask.

Grant shrugs. "Whatever capacity you'll have us. Colleagues, acquaintances, friends, lovers."

Alice can't pretend she's not tempted by the offer. It wouldn't take much for their meal to be one thousand percent better than what she was going to cobble together with her sparse groceries and mostly dry ingredients. She could probably make a cabbage soup, but that's only if the cabbage in the fridge hasn't wilted already, which is very likely that it has. . .

"Maybe," she says. She's too hungry and tired right now to say no outright. "I'll think about it."

When Grant pulls the car up to her apartment, she's about to say her quick thanks before basically ducking and rolling out of the moving vehicle when she does a double take at a couple standing outside of her building, one ringing the buzzer repeatedly.

Alice lowers the window and leans outside. "Olivia?!"

Her sister and her mate turn around to look at Alice and Grant, and Alice's jaw hangs open. "What the hell?"

"Al!" Olivia calls and runs up to the side of the car, nearly slipping on the slushy sidewalk. "We've been waiting for you."

"Wh—"

"And just who is this?" Olivia extends an arm into the car through the open window. Grant, ever quick on his feet, puts the car into park and shakes her outstretched hand. "Olivia Walton, Alice's favorite sister."

"My only sister," Alice cuts in, to Grant's ever-growing charm and amusement.

"Grant Thompson, Alice's favorite coworker. Thrilled to meet you."

Alice gets out of the car to give her sister a long hug before also embracing her brother-in-law Jonathan. He introduces himself to Grant while Alice lightly pulls her sister's hair which is tied in one smooth braid over her shoulder. She's always coveted Olivia's perfectly smooth auburn hair. "What are you doing here?"

"Keeping you company," Olivia knocks some fresh snow off of Alice's shoulder. "You can't be alone for Thanksgiving."

Alice hugs her sister again, tighter this time, touched that she would sacrifice time with the whole family to be with her in the city. "I love you."

"I know, I know. I love you, too. Now, can we sleep on your pull-out tonight? The hotel situation was dire."

Alice laughs and now notices the suitcase and duffle bag stacked by her building door. "Of course. Fair warning, I have nothing planned, so takeout is on the menu for tomorrow."

"Takeout is perfect," Olivia says and turns over her shoulder to where Grant and Johnathan watch the reunion. "What are your plans for the holiday, Grant?"

"I'm planning on setting the record of most slices of pie eaten in one sitting. We would love to have the three of you if you're free," Grant says, ever polite, ever the most charming fucking person Alice has ever met.

"Yes!" Olivia says at the same time Alice says, "Maybe."

Olivia turns to her younger sister, "You heard your favorite co-worker, there will be enough pie to make a contest of eating slices. We have to go."

Olivia sends Alice a look that she recognizes from their whole lives, the one that says *you better do this or so help me I will tell Mom what you did and you will never see the TV again.* Alice swallows a sigh and gives a shallow nod. "We'll be there."

Grant's face lights up, and for a moment, Alice thinks the potential anguish of being with her scent matches and their families on Thanksgiving might just be worth it to see him smile like that.

"Great! Okay, wow. Great." Grant reaches out and squeezes Alice's shoulder. His touch through three layers of clothing still feels exhilarating for Alice, despite having *just* made out with him. "Caleb will be thrilled. He's, um, yeah, he's going to be excited."

Alice shivers, whether from the snow or the way Grant's voice sounds like he just won a prize, she's not sure.

"We should go inside," she says and looks to Olivia for help.

"Right. Grant, it was so great to meet you. I am looking forward to seeing how many pieces of pie you can put away."

"Me, too." Grant gives Alice one last look before retreating to his still-running car, the exhaust pipe letting out a steady stream of condensation.

Alice bustles Olivia and Johnathan into the building before they can try to talk to Grant more through his open car window, or wave him on his way like parents watching their son drive off to college.

"Is he your scent match?" Jonathan asks because obviously Olivia's secret keeping can only be expected to go so far.

"One of them," Alice sighs. "I've been trying to keep my distance."

They stomp up one flight of stairs and then another on their way to the fourth floor.

"God, why?" Jonathan asks, like the thought pains him to even consider. "Don't you want to be near them?"

"No," she says, but the churning of her stomach when facing another night alone tells a different story. "I don't need a pack, I'm only twenty-six."

Jonathan looks at Alice like she's unstable. He's a year younger than her, but he met Olivia two years before when he was halfway through his history master's program.

Olivia was looking for an Omega, Jonathan was sick of relying on heat clinics every few months, they met on one of the apps, and the rest is history. They love each other deeply and were bonded within two months, married officially a year later. A perfect pack of two.

"Are you at least letting them court you?" Olivia asks as they reach Alice's door.

"Well I'm not. . . *not* letting them court me," she says. Ignoring all of their messages and invitations isn't exactly being the most receptive to it, but it's not like she's turning away the free food that appears on her desk, or sending back the three teeny tiny horse toys that showed up yesterday with her other mini desk animals. "I let Grant drive me home today."

Olivia deposits her duffle on the ground next to the couch and asks, "And would you have gone to their Thanksgiving if I didn't say yes?"

"Maybe," she says. "I'm not sure, but yeah, maybe."

"Have you been sleeping? You look exhausted," Jonathan says. He, like her sister, has barely a filter when it comes to talking to Alice.

"Probably because she's ignoring her mates."

"They're not my mates."

"But they *are* your scent matches," Olivia says. She hangs her and Johnathan's coats on the hooks by the front door. Alice hands over her coat, but keeps the red scarf looped around her neck. "Let's let that piece of information sink in, shall we? Two. Scent. Matches."

"I know," Alice drops onto the couch and stuffs her face in her hands. Her tiny one-bedroom doesn't feel big enough for the three of them and all of her conflicted emotions. "I'm just—"

"Not ready?" Olivia asks.

"Scared?" Jonathan offers.

"Tired," Alice adds definitely. Olivia and Johnathan both soften at this admission. The last two weeks have turned her life on its head. She met her scent matches, went through an eight-day heat, and worked thirty-three hours in three days, of course she's exhausted.

Olivia puts a hand on her sister's shoulder and squeezes three times. The family code. *I love you,* those squeezes say; *I've got you. I see you. I'm with you.*

Alice covers her sister's hand with her own and squeezes three times back.

"I think I'm going to try to sleep for a few hours if that's okay with you two," Alice says. "I'm sorry I can't be more entertaining tonight."

"Don't worry about it," Olivia says. "We'll raid your fridge and take advantage of your Netflix subscription."

Alice gives her sister and brother-in-law one more hug each before slinking to her room, kicking off her slacks, unclasping her bra, and falling straight into bed, the red scarf still keeping her warm and offering some semblance of comfort while her heart constricts in a confusing strain.

ten

ALICE, Olivia, and Johnathan order a car to Caleb and Grant's. The heating went out in the entire apartment building in the middle of the night, and they're too cold to even consider walking to a bus stop.

Alice wiggles her toes in her boots in the warm car as the nice man prattles on about the holiday and how Thanksgiving was much better than Christmas, but only if you preferred turkey to ham, which he did.

Alice's apartment is nice enough—a one bedroom with a small dishwasher which made the place worth its weight in gold, she thought—and cheap. But it was never lacking in maintenance issues. Leaky window wells on rainy days, no central air conditioning, a barely functioning elevator, and the occasional heat system failure were all just part of the charm. Charming until, of course, Alice had guests who thought huddling around a space heater with various electric and microwavable heating pads was not as fun and delightful as being somewhere cozy might be.

She could afford somewhere nicer, but it felt like an

unnecessary expense when it was just her here. Plus it allowed her to save lots of money.

The superintendent said the heat would come back on this afternoon, but Alice had to agree that spending some hours in Grant and Caleb's warm home would be a better alternative to shivering over a bowl of spaghetti and meatballs.

So, they burned some cornbread muffins—Olivia's fault, she is always so wary of raw baked goods—and made their way to Caleb and Grant's townhouse.

A sweet-looking Omega woman ushers them into the house, introducing herself as Molly and immediately fawning over Alice, saying how lovely it was that she could make it. She goes on about how she can see why the boys are so fond of her because, "You are beautiful, just radiant."

Alice does not feel radiant, especially next to her sister, who is like a sleeker, better-dressed, more emotionally mature version of herself, but she takes the compliment and lets Molly pull her into a hug in the entryway.

Molly must already know that Caleb and Grant want Alice to join their pack, but Alice just hopes that she doesn't know the *real* reason Grant and Caleb are so fond of her. Namely that she made them knot her multiple times a day for over a week while she languished in a feverish first heat. Oh, and the fact that they are scent matches. That discovery would go over well and wouldn't derail conversations whatsoever.

"Mom, unhand our guest, please," Caleb says. He's wearing a black apron over a cozy sweater and slacks, a look that shouldn't make Alice's mouth go dry, but does nonetheless.

She sees right away that he and Grant have hung up the photos since she was here last and unpacked more of the boxes that were around pushed against the walls. The place feels cozy now, homey, and it's filled with nearly a dozen bodies now that they've joined the fray. It looks already too crowded to add Alice, Olivia, and Johnathan to the mix, but the quiet relief on Caleb's face is proof enough that he at least wants her there.

He looks tired, too. She recognizes how he feels like a mirror, the weariness in his spine from lack of sleep.

"We brought cornbread," Alice says after they've quietly stared at each other for a few moments. Caleb glances down at the paper plate of yellow muffins made from a box mix, a fact Alice or Olivia would never admit to their mother. "Just a little burnt."

"I love cornbread," Caleb says, and takes the plate from her. His fingers linger and burn on the back of her hand as he grabs the plate, but she doesn't want to pull away from the touch. "They're perfect."

"I agree," Olivia chimes in. Caleb looks at her like he's just realized there's more than one person in this front room. "You must be Caleb, nice to meet you."

"And you, Olivia." Caleb offers Olivia a handshake due to the appraising look on her sister's face, Alice knows it's a good one.

Grant thumps down the stairs with a clean-shaven jaw wearing a dark green button-up and embraces Olivia and Johnathan like they're long-time friends instead of being practically strangers who've met for a grand total of three minutes. He pulls Alice in for a hug, too, and his scent sinks right into her.

She pulls away quicker than her body would like, but she's trying to maintain the feeble semblance of control she has over herself when Grant or Caleb are in touching distance.

Additional introductions are made as they're bustled into the central part of the house, Caleb's mom, Molly, and his two Alpha dads, Dean and Marcus, are all accounted for in the living room with Grant's Beta parents, Tara and Luke, as well. It's a lot of names for an overwhelmed Alice, but she makes it a point to repeat them in her mind ten times over.

Grant and Caleb introduce Alice as their coworker, the workhorse of the marketing team who makes their job easy every day. She doesn't add any extra context about their relationship and if that hurts their feelings, they don't let on. Alice is exceptionally curious about farming and sits herself next to Caleb's dads to ask what the pumpkin farming industry is like until dinner is ready to be served.

Around the dining table, Alice sits with Caleb to her left, Grant right across from her, and Olivia at her right, whispering crass things about her scent matches.

"They can *cook*, and they're *homeowners,* and they're fucking *hot,* Al," Olivia insists.

Alice kicks her sister's leg under the table, not for the first time today.

The food looks as decadent as it smells, but what is added to the indelible comfort of the homemade feast in front of them is the perfect scent of Caleb and Grant's home. It's warm, like them. Familiar.

Alarm bells should be blaring in her head, but she's too tired and hungry to give it much thought. Right now, her top priority is digging into some turkey slathered in the homemade cranberry sauce that is set in front of her.

"This looks unbelievably delicious," Olivia adds to the chorus of praise.

"Caleb has been slaving over it all day," Grant says. "He's a great cook."

"You made all of this?" Alice asks, and his cheeks pink just a touch.

"I had lots of help," he says. He's scooping servings of food onto her plate without asking, and she doesn't tell him to stop. "My mom made the potatoes, the rolls are Luke's masterpiece, and Grant made two pies."

"Well, it all looks. . . wow," Alice sits up taller.

"Thank you for having us. It's nice to be with good people and great food," Olivia says, already digging in on her own plate. "Plus your heater is working."

Alice doles out another kick, but Olivia doesn't even flinch.

"What happened to your heater?" Grant asks, pausing his work pouring sparkling punch from a pitcher into glasses for everyone.

"It went out last night in the whole building," Olivia says. "Guess it happens all the time."

"Only sometimes. Rarely," Alice hurries to add. "Twice a year, maybe."

"You must have been freezing!" Molly exclaims.

"Well, she has a space heater," Jonathan adds. "And many blankets."

"Many," Alice agrees.

Caleb scoops cranberry sauce onto her plate and she lightly touches his wrist before he can put the spoon back in the bowl. He adds another big scoop and she nods.

"When will it be fixed?" Grant asks, his voice too distressed for a peaceful family dinner.

"Some time today, I think," Alice says. "We'll be fine."

"You should stay here tonight," Grant says. "We have a guest room. And a pullout couch."

"What a generous offer!" Olivia perks up, and Alice would kick her sister again, but everyone at the table is talking about how great of an idea that is, especially with all the snow falling this week.

"You've got a full house already," Alice says. "We don't want to impose."

"No imposition," Caleb says. He grabs a glass of sparkling punch from Grant and places it in front of Alice before he starts working on his own plate. "Grant's parents live downtown and mine decided to stay in a hotel."

"It has a spa. And a hot tub," Molly interjects.

"Fortuitous," Olivia says. *Fucking traitor*. "We would love that. Right?"

Alice puts on a stellar performance of someone who doesn't want to commit sororicide.

"Right," Alice says, then digs into her heaping plate of food.

"So, Alice, how do you like working with the boys?" Molly jumps in, changing the subject.

It's a welcome distraction from the previous topic and the impending slumber party, though Alice's neck heats thinking about all the ways they've . . . *worked together* since they started.

She says, "They're great. Very professional."

"She's lying, she hated me at first," Caleb says.

"She did," Grant agrees. Even Olivia nods. Alice sputters before pulling herself together enough to defend herself.

"It was a misunderstanding," Alice says. "I thought *he* didn't like me. He doesn't use exclamation points."

"Horrible bedside manner," one of Caleb's dads, Dean, she thinks, remarks solemnly.

"We work in an office, not a hospital. I'm not even client-facing, really," Caleb says.

"Well, that's probably because you don't use any exclamation points," Molly says. Caleb looks around the table like he's in an episode of *The Twilight Zone*.

"Knucklehead son aside, how is it?" Marcus asks.

"Just fine," Alice says, then pulls a face like she's weighing the truth of that. "Well, I mean, it's okay. I like most of the people I work with, but the job itself is . . . it can be demanding."

"She means her dick boss takes advantage of her kindness," Olivia translates.

"Constantly," Grant agrees.

"I've been telling her she should find a new job," Olivia says. "Any marketing agency would be lucky to have her."

"That is true," Caleb says.

Alice's head swivels back and forth between everyone talking about how bad her job is. Part of her has known that this job isn't sustainable for her, but another, much larger part has told her not to look for something better. Her current job is safe. There aren't any Alphas or Omegas to sniff out what she is—well, that's been the case until recently.

She has a set of tasks that she's good at and a team she likes pretty well. If she went somewhere else it would be less predictable and had the chance to be just as bad, if not worse, in terms of workload. And if it was worse, she wouldn't even have Lily to hang out and commiserate with.

It all feels like a risk to even think about it too closely.

Sensing Alice's discomfort, Grant's mom, Tara asks, "Have you been with the company long?"

"I started when I finished college, so just about four years now."

The team of parents all wear surprised looks, but Molly is the first to ask, "How old are you, sweetheart?"

"Twenty-six," Alice says, and Caleb's fathers pause over their meals.

Molly doesn't miss a beat, though, and if she's shocked that a twenty-six-year-old Omega is unmated, she hides it well.

"I loved twenty-six," Tara says and squeezes her husband's hand on the table. "The year I met Luke."

Grant looks at Alice across the table for a beat while the conversation carries on around them to different topics. His eyes tell too much—they're open and expressive, plaintive and hungry. She chews her food thoroughly, sips at the punch, and eventually, has to look away.

* * *

After dinner, there's so, so much pie, followed by a couple of hours of relaxing. The super still hasn't emailed to say that the heater is fixed, but even if he had, Alice doesn't know that she could pry herself off of this couch that she seems to sink further into with each passing moment.

An old Christmas Rom-Com plays quietly over the television, one of her favorites, but her eyes grow too heavy to watch. Caleb and Grant's parents made their exit half an hour ago, while Grant offered to drive Alice's sister and brother-in-law back to the apartment to pick up some clothes.

Alice, warm beneath a soft heated blanket that smells just like Grant and Caleb, was more than glad she stayed behind.

"Alice," Caleb whispers, kneeling in front of her.

She'd drifted to sleep briefly, she wasn't sure how long, but Caleb had changed into plaid pants and a navy sweatshirt in the meantime. His hair is damp, too, and he smells like his tea tree shampoo which makes her lips curl into a small, sleepy smile.

"Hm?"

"I said I brought you some pajamas." Caleb holds up some clothes.

"Too tired," Alice says, then pulls the blanket closer.

"You don't want to sleep in jeans." He's stern, eyebrows set and face oh, so serious. His way or the highway, and all that.

Caleb laughs through his nose, a little huff at the words Alice didn't think she'd spoken out loud. "Sure, sure, come on. Up."

Alice groans but lets Caleb pull her to her feet, he steadies her with a hand on her waist. She blinks a few times, the grogginess lessening only to realize how very close they're standing to each other. She watches his Adam's apple move down his wide throat with a swallow, and feels his thumb glide across a slice of bare skin exposed on her hip.

Her eyes are at the perfect height to stare right at his lips, which look smooth and soft.

"Thank you for coming today," Caleb says, his voice tenderly quiet. He leans forward just a bit, enough that his mouth is practically hovering over hers.

"Thank you for having us," she says. Her eyes flutter shut against her will and Caleb presses his warm lips to the side of her mouth before pulling away.

"You should change," he says, voice lower than usual. Alice opens her eyes and nods, coming back to herself.

Damn hormones.

"Right." She grabs the clothes from his outstretched hand, careful not to touch his skin, and retreats to the downstairs bathroom where she wets her hands with cold water and presses them to her heated neck. She's fine. This is fine. They could sleep in the same house and not sleep together, they were adults after all, and Grant would be back with Olivia and Johnathan any second now.

It was good of him to pull away.

She repeats all this in her mind while pulling on a long sleeve and sweats, both belonging to Caleb, if the scent was anything to go by.

Because she can't help herself, she takes a moment to peer into the drawers and under the sink. Sunscreen, towels, some boxes of toothpaste—nothing exceptionally interesting. Usual guest bathroom fare. What she really wants is to poke around their closet and bedroom. She wouldn't dare though, she knows about curiosity killing cats and the like.

With her own clothes folded neatly in a pile—bra stuffed in between her folded-up jeans because the thought of him seeing her bra was laughably making her skin hot to the touch—she makes her way back to the living room where Caleb now sits on the edge of the folded-out couch bed, his elbows on his knees.

She'd already decided that Olivia and Johnathan would take the guest bed and she'd take the couch bed. The other bed in the house was *not* going to be an option.

"Did you find what you were looking for?"

"Hm?"

"In the bathroom?" Caleb looks like the question is genuine and not like he expects that she was snooping for no reason. "I heard the drawer."

"Oh, definitely. Yes, I uh, just needed some floss," she lies. "Stuck food, and all that."

"Good. I hope that's enough blankets," he nods his head

over at the made-up bed, the top two are ones she recognizes from her heat.

"Looks great."

Alice holds her elbow, ever aware of the awkward air between them, but unsure how to address it. His phone rings before she has to, the ringtone breaking through the quiet making both of them jump. Caleb pulls it from his pocket.

"It's Grant," he says to Alice before answering. "You okay?"

Alice can't hear what Grant says through the phone and she tries to make it look like she's not actively trying to eavesdrop. Caleb gives a few one-word responses as Grant speaks before saying he'll see him soon, he loves him, then ends the call.

"Your heater is fixed," Caleb says.

"Oh," Alice says. "That's. . . good news."

"It is," Caleb agrees, then after a minute remembers to add, "Your sister and her husband said they wanted to just stay there for the night."

Alice feels a longing pull to the sofa bed. She's already so cozy and her bones are weary and exhausted, but if her heater is fixed then they probably want her to go home, too, right?

They remain standing there, so stiff across from each other.

Alice steels herself. "I'd like to stay. Since the bed's already made up and everything."

Caleb grimaces.

"Unless you want me to go," Alice is quick to add.

"No, no, I just hadn't even considered you going home. Of course you can stay. I want you to."

"Okay." Alice sits right down on the edge of the sofa

bed, decision made, no need to beg. "I guess I'll head to sleep then—"

"Can I hold you?" Caleb blurts. At Alice's frozen expression, he rakes a hand through his hair and goes on. "I haven't been sleeping really, is all, and I thought maybe if I could. . . hold you, and just. . . be near you it might help. Just for a while, no funny business."

Confirming that he hadn't been sleeping well is almost comforting; she feels less lonely to know she's not the only one struggling since the night after her heat broke.

"No funny business," Alice repeats.

She doesn't tell Caleb how bad of an idea it probably is, or give him the fifteen reasons flashing through her mind not to. Instead, she just crawls onto the sofa bed and under the comforter, sheet, and blankets. Once she's in, Alice lifts her head to look at Caleb, then pats the bed next to her.

He scrambles in, the springs squeak under his weight before he lies down beneath the covers and gathers her to him. After some adjusting, his arms wrap around her, one on the back of her head, and her face is to his chest. Right where she can scent him and where, after a few breaths, she feels a low purr emanating from his chest.

"I'm glad you came today," Caleb says. "I missed you."

"What did you miss?" she asks. "My bad grammar?"

Caleb laughs, his chest shaking against her, and she feels his lips press against her head.

"You do have bad grammar sometimes," he says. "I'm sorry I wasn't kinder when I started at Labyrinth, and I guess all of the time. I don't mean to be so. . . intense."

"You are intense," she agrees, and his chest shakes again. He pulls her closer to him and she lets him, sinking into it. "I was wrong and defensive and didn't think you liked me, and I hate when people don't like me."

"Who doesn't like you?"

"Well, you, I thought, for one," Alice says. She remembers the cold rooftop where she accused him of just that, when the fire of her heat was brimming beneath her skin waiting to be set off. It feels like months have passed since then. "Probably lots of other people, too."

"I don't think so," Caleb says. He sounds tired, more relaxed than usual. "I liked you right away. From your first email, you delighted me. You're kind to everyone, even when they take advantage of you. And you're smart, hard-working, and very, very beautiful."

She's glad he can't see her face, all tucked up under his chin as she is. Alice has never been able to hide her blush.

"And then I came to the office and there you were. I started missing you as soon as I met you," he says. "I never want you to leave."

The words are melting into her, she can't even find it in herself to feel the wriggling dread when she's pressed against Caleb like this.

"I didn't even mean to find you," Caleb says, but his voice is heavy with sleep. "You snuck up on me."

Gradually her muscles unclench until she is a pool of warmth and relaxation all wrapped up in Caleb Everett, her self-declared work nemesis and begrudging scent match.

They both fall swiftly to sleep.

eleven

ALICE'S SKIN is warm when she wakes again, her neck still stuffed into the crook of Caleb's neck. His legs are slung over hers, limbs all tangled up in each other, but there's an undeniable need washing its way through her body.

It doesn't feel like her heat did. That was frantic and desperate, this was a slow building thrum between her thighs and in her chest.

Alice wiggles closer, just the slightest rub of her front against his, and Caleb lets out a sleepy sigh. She doesn't know how long she's been asleep, though the moon still shines through the tall windows making rectangles slant on the walls.

Her back arches, pressing her chest even closer to his, and this time she feels part of him stiffening against her. There is a place in her brain that knows this is a poor idea—waking him up for sex would send the exact message that she's set out *not* to deliver, but his scent wrapped up with hers and their bodies being glued together is messing with her critical thinking and reasoning ability.

She needs him. He's here, and she has to have him.

"Caleb," she whispers and slides a hand under his shirt.

"Hm?" his eyes stay closed, but his breathing speeds up as he wakes up. Alice rubs her thighs together, the slight friction doing nothing to ease her want.

"Caleb," she says again, and this time it's a plea. His eyes fly open then, his grip tightening on her.

"What's the matter?" He smooths a hand over her hair, pushing some behind her ear.

"I want you," she admits. "Please."

In the low light, Alice sees a muscle in Caleb's jaw flex.

"Are you sure?" he asks.

What a gentleman.

To show just how sure she is, Alice grabs Caleb's hand and slides it down her stomach and beneath the band of the sweatpants she wears. Her slick coats his fingers as soon as his fingers find their mark and they both shudder ragged breaths.

"Take these off," Caleb growls without hesitation, and suddenly, both of them are wiggling out of their clothes. Pants and shirts are tossed to the floor before crashing back into each other with feverish hands roaming across expanses of bare skin. His hands move like he wants to touch all of her at once.

He squeezes her breasts and pulls at her nipples until they're hard, all while kissing her lips, cheeks, jaw, down her neck, and across her collarbone. When he kisses her chest and takes one of her nipples into his mouth, Alice gasps and her slick coats the insides of her thighs.

She doesn't have to tell him to touch her there, he knows what she needs. His long fingers dance along her stomach before delving between her legs. He moans when he sinks one finger inside of her. If she'd intended to keep quiet, there's no possibility of that now.

"You must know how obscene this is," Caleb says. "Your cunt on my fingers, wet and hot and fucking made for me, for us."

"Show me," Alice says, then maneuvers herself to climb atop him. "Show me how it's made for you."

"*Christ.*" Caleb helps pull her over him and in doing so, Alice has a clear shot of Grant behind the couch, his silhouette prominent beneath the light that is coming through the windows. He's shirtless, his hair looks tousled as if he was just asleep. His boxers are inched down his hips so that his cock can hang over the band, thick and hard as he strokes the shaft. He really is massive, all of him. Alice holds a hand out towards him, beckoning in any way she can.

It takes no prodding before Grant crawls onto the sofa bed, his body filling the space she just vacated. Caleb groans at the sight of him and pulls Grant's face down to his for an open-mouthed kiss that only makes Alice wetter.

Unable to wait a moment more, Alice grips Caleb's cock and lines it up at her entrance. He freezes and Grant pulls back from the kiss to watch. She rubs his head back and forth along herself, the slick coating it and mixing with the pre-cum there. Then she starts to descend onto it, just the head, the intrusion already delicious inside of her. Three shaky breaths release as Alice sinks further down onto Caleb. It's a relief as much as it is an anguish to be filled like that, the top of his knot stretching, begging to be let in.

After a steadying moment in silence, Alice rolls her hips. She hasn't done this in a while, rode someone like this, but her body remembers what to do. Caleb groans like she's afflicted him in the most perfect, sinful way.

"Alice. My perfect Alice," Caleb says.

"Go ahead, baby, show us how you ride him," Grant says. His hand is already back on his dick, eyes locked on where she and Caleb are fused together. "I promise he'll fill you up right."

Alice needs no more encouragement from there. She leans forward, dropping her hands on Caleb's shoulders, and grinds her hips up and down the length of him, pushing a little deeper with every stroke.

Caleb's hands settle on her hips, fingers digging into the soft skin of her ass as she rides him. It's easier to fall into them like this, in the cover of the night without the harsh reality of day around her. She loses herself to the rhythm of taking Caleb, the tiny moans she breathes into his ear mingled with the sound of his own.

Grant watches them with embers simmering behind his eyes, pumping his dick into his fist like it's the single best show he's ever seen.

"You're beautiful," Caleb breathes. "God, you're the most beautiful thing I've ever seen, Alice."

His voice is labored, and as she takes him even deeper, his knot stretches her entrance. A moan breaks free from his chest and his hips begin their own work moving into her. It hits inside her at a new angle, deeper than it had just been, slamming against that spot inside her that makes her shake. The sensations overwhelm her, and she lets him take over, rutting into her cunt while she can only let out breathy, high-pitched moans in his ear.

Grant is running a hand over her back and muttering a string of filth to them both, to Caleb about how he fills their mate so well, knows exactly what to give her and just how to give it to her, and to Alice about how perfect she is for them, how they were made for one another, made to make each other feel exactly the way they're feeling now. In the movement of the moment—their scents a heady cloud around them and their bodies moving seamlessly with each other—she's inclined to believe him.

She is so close, right on the brink of that explosive release no man had taken her to before them, and when Caleb's knot breaches her entrance entirely, she comes on a shout, clutching him as he does her. His knot swells inside of her, locking them together and the squeeze of her orgasm sends Caleb right into his own, stuffing her full of his release. She grinds her hips against him still, the pressure on her clit making her orgasm go, and go, as her nails dig half-moons into his shoulders.

Grant's moans grow closer together, more frantic, and it's as if Caleb can read Grant's mind because just as Grant begins to shift on the bed beside them, Caleb turns his neck and opens his mouth wide. Like a choreographed dance perfected over many years of practice, Grant holds behind Caleb's head so tenderly as he pushes his cock into Caleb's mouth, pumping a few times before bursting.

Alice watches Caleb's throat work as he swallows him down and she moans again, bringing her fingers to her clit to rub herself to another orgasm as she watches them. It takes barely anything to get her there, and before Grant's cock is out of Caleb's mouth, she's squeezing around his knot all over again.

She comes down at the same time Grant does, and she can't help but seal her lips first to Grant's in a sloppy kiss before doing the same to Caleb. He tastes like the load he'd just taken so well, like the best fucking boy she'd ever seen, and it's so lewd to taste Grant on his tongue.

"Share," Caleb says, and Alice is quick to oblige, making Grant taste his own come on her tongue, then on Caleb's. She feels like this could go on all night, the messy ministering of tongues and lips and hands between each other, but the heavy weight of satisfied exhaustion settles on her and their kisses and touches grow more languid. She lays on Caleb's front, still stuck together as his knot shrinks inside of her, and Grant lies next to them with his hand tracing circles on Alice's back.

Alone in the dark like this, still hours to sunrise, she is perfectly peaceful. She can't worry about this being a poor idea, or about what it will mean when she wakes up tomorrow when she can dissect everything in the harsh light of the sun.

She feels only the heat of Grant and Caleb, the content purring from their chests lulling her right back to that peaceful sleep she only gets with them around.

The rest will have to wait until tomorrow.

twelve

WHEN TOMORROW COMES, she wakes past noon, Caleb still knocked out beside her. They're sprawled naked beneath the blankets, his leg over hers with her arm slung over his chest. She never thought she'd find chest hair hot, but whatever he's got going on here is definitely working for her.

She rubs her eyes a bit and then pushes her head up to see into the kitchen where Grant is cooking something for once—pancakes, from the smell of it. Both of them have messy hair, no evidence of their perfectly put-together office looks. Caleb wakes with a big inhale and pulls Alice to his chest. He puts his face in her neck and kisses her there three times before just holding her, both of them joining the world of the living by degrees.

"I have to get up," Alice says.

Caleb groans and pulls her tighter to him. "Five more minutes."

"I have to pee," she says.

He relaxes his arms around her, enough for her to wiggle away from him. "Can't fight biology," he says.

Alice pauses before grabbing her clothes and scurrying out of the room and to the bathroom down the hall. She definitely *wasn't* fighting her biological urges when she woke up in the middle of the night and pounced on Caleb like a feral cat. God, what was she thinking? Every time she let herself have them, it was going to make it that much harder to cut them off entirely, and it's prudent that she do just that.

Her face flushes remembering all of it. Alice isn't a stranger to sex, even good sex, she's had a small share of, but she isn't accustomed to sex like *that*. The kind that makes her feel woozy and overwhelmed, a zap to all of her senses. If they could keep doing that without any pesky strings attached, she would be thrilled.

But sex with Caleb and Grant isn't just sex; they want her in their pack as their mates, and they've made themselves abundantly clear about this.

She wants. . . She doesn't quite know what she wants.

It feels disingenuous to say that she wants nothing to do with them. It is also disingenuous for her to say that she doesn't want what they want, the love and companionship that comes with a pack, a family. But how can she possibly have that while still keeping what she's worked so hard for?

Grant and Caleb are muttering something to each other when she pads back into the kitchen. The two of them are so beautiful, it still almost takes her breath away to look at them and have them look back at her. But how they stand in front of her right now, she feels particularly lucky.

Caleb's terse demeanor and seriousness at work is belied by his quiet laughs and complete earnestness. The way his crooked bottom teeth press into his lip when he's listening, and even the flush of his cheeks when she's near him endear him to her.

He watches her, observes, orders her favorite food, and puts little horse figurines on her desk when she isn't looking. Grant, too, is so much like an affectionate puppy that will do anything to make them happy—but he's the quiet strength here.

He is the true Alpha of the pack, confident and steady whereas Caleb is careful and wary, and Alice can see herself fit right between them perfectly; even with all of her jagged, people-pleasing edges.

There's a reason they're her scent matches.

But how could she commit to this? How could anyone see their perfect, balanced relationship and decide it would be simple to join them? A relationship with one person was hard enough, to add another into the mix and everything hinges on emotional communication and honesty. Alice is good at many, many things, but sharing her feelings like that isn't one of them. She can't even tell others who she really is, her closest friend still thinks she's a Beta.

She would disappoint them, and by then, she'd love them fully, and hurting them would break her.

She can't do this.

"I, uh," Alice clears her throat and the two of them turn quickly to her with smiles warm as the sun. "I think I should go."

Caleb's face falls. Grant remains calm.

"Are you hungry? You should eat," Grant says.

"No," Alice responds, though her stomach growling at the smell of the breakfast would indicate otherwise. "It's just... my sister is in town for a few more days and I should be with her."

"Right," Grant says. His eyes narrow on her, but he doesn't disagree. Caleb, on the other hand, moves around the counter to hover next to her.

"Is this about last night?" he says. "Because if it is, I'm sorry, I should've—I don't know—kept my hands to myself. I shouldn't have—"

"It's not that," Alice says. "You didn't do anything wrong. If anything, I instigated."

"Tell us, then," Grant says. His voice is so level, but there's a storm behind those gray eyes. "Why are you so keen to run out of here as soon as the light of day has touched this?"

"Because there is no *this*. There is you two, and there is me. And I'm grateful for all of the orgasms, but they don't change anything."

The sizzling and popping of bacon on the pan behind Grant is the only sound while her words settle into everyone's brains. She regrets them instantly, but doesn't say so.

"She's afraid," Grant says. He's all disappointed and crossed arms, it makes her feel three feet tall and like a pane of glass, he can stare right through.

"I'm not," Alice says with a crack in her voice.

"What are you afraid of?" Caleb asks. "Is it us? Do you think you'd be unhappy?"

"No, you're both so—" Alice runs a hand down her face then holds her neck. "You're lovely and kind and hardworking, and it's obvious you love each other very much, but I just don't think I can fit into this."

"What do you mean?" Caleb asks, and steps closer still. "You're exactly what we need, Alice, we've been waiting to find you."

"That's just it. You've been waiting to find an *Omega*. Not *me*."

Both men stare at Alice, not comprehending what she means.

"It's in your nature to want an Omega. One that you can

take care of and fill with little fucking handsome babies—*of course* you've been waiting to find an Omega. But can either of you tell me honestly that if we weren't scent matches you'd have even considered me an option?"

They blink for a moment, and Caleb's mouth hangs open like he wants to say something, but he can't find the words.

"Admit it. You aren't *choosing* me, something made that choice for you. And whether that was destiny or biology, how can I ever trust that either of you like me for who I am and not just *what* I am?"

"Sweetheart," Caleb whispers. Every emotion is evident on his face.

"That's what this is about? You think we don't like you for who you are, that we aren't attracted to you as a human being?" Grant asks. "We've been working with you for *months*, Alice, it's not like you're a stranger, *of course* we like you as a person."

"And this feels right, doesn't it? You have to feel it," Caleb says.

That's the scariest part of all this, Alice decides. The fact that she does feel it. There's an urge when she's with them to stay there, and when she's not, she wants to get back to them as soon as possible. There's an unsteadiness in her at the thought of them not being already bonded to her, and the impulse to vomit at the thought of them bonding with anyone else. She's been battling this incessant feeling that they're *hers* and that none of them can belong to anyone other than each other.

"You haven't been sleeping," Caleb says after she's been quiet for too long. "Me either. And Grant has been a mess, grumpy and restless, but last night I slept. And when I woke up, I felt awake for the first time in days. You too, I can see it on your face."

"We're no good when we're apart," Grant agrees.

"Well, we need to learn to be!" Alice spouts.

She calms her breath in the quiet that follows, then meets both of their eyes, first Grant, then Caleb. He looks like a particularly sad small animal that's just been kicked.

"Yes, I'm fucking scared," she admits. "I don't know that I'll ever be the Omega you two want, and I don't think I can take it if you learn everything there is to know about me and decide you don't want me."

"Isn't that what a relationship is? Learning every little thing about a person and choosing to love them anyway?" Caleb asks.

"Give us the chance to choose you, too," Grant says.

Alice wants to go to them and let them wrap her in their arms and hold her and kiss her and tell her everything will be okay for them. She wants to believe they'll be patient with her and love her, even if she's headstrong and skips lunch and is late constantly.

Caleb closes the distance between them and pulls her lightly towards him. She doesn't fight him.

"Please consider it." Caleb kisses her on the head like it's the most natural thing in the world, then rests his head against hers. "Don't rule us out."

Grant stays where he is, his face like stone, but resigned. He gives a nod finally, agreeing with Caleb. "We'll be here to prove it to you."

thirteen

THE NEXT WEEK at work is a total shit show for Alice, and she suspects the same is true for Caleb and Grant —the three of them have a matching set of bags beneath their eyes. And although work has been moving on as usual, none of them have appeared at all cheerful about it.

When Logan tried to pawn off two more projects on Alice this week, she politely told him she didn't have the bandwidth, which astonished him, but he didn't press. She was glad she held her ground, even if she almost started crying in the bathroom afterward. Caleb, though, had a smirk on his face when she passed by him.

Grant was right when he said that they were no good when Alice was forcing distance between them. It was so sudden, the shift from not wanting them at all to wanting them all the time. In the office, she gravitated towards them, like there was a subtle pull to their desks, a simple comfort when they passed by her or leaned over her chair to review something on her monitor.

Little gifts have still showed up on her desk, like a bagel with almond spread from the place that she likes so much.

Occasionally, a Tupperware with something homemade and delicious for lunch.

Conversations have stayed only about work and glances remain pained and lingering.

Olivia is no longer trying to convince her to call them, giving Alice the time she needs to argue internally with herself. Their mother, though, has not been quite as patient. One of Alice's dads bought her a plane ticket home for Christmas, and while she's planning on going, the thought of being even farther from Caleb and Grant makes her skin crawl.

The problem is this: she wants to believe them.

Every day she gets closer to being theirs, and the feeling of inevitability terrifies her. Of course, she wants them, she's been a mess without them. A not-so-insignificant part of her wants to try making a relationship work, but then she talks herself so far out of it to a point she's amazed she even considered it at all. The cycle repeats every day. Twelve times minimum.

Sitting at lunch on Friday with Lily, Alice tries to listen to her friend talk about the latest book she's reading. As Lily debates with herself the physics of a particular sex scene between a Kraken and a human in said book, Alice sits up straight, an idea strikes her like lightning.

"What's the matter?" Lily whispers, all monster physics forgotten.

"I need to tell you something. Two somethings. Well, three."

Lily blinks her big eyes and puts her spoon down. "Go on."

"Grant and Caleb are Alphas," Alice says. Lily gets that look like juicy gossip is about to drop, and she has no fucking idea just *how* juicy. "I know this because they're my scent matches."

Lily freezes, processes, buffers, then processes again. She tilts her head and purses her lips.

"I'm an Omega," Alice fills in the blanks.

"Holy shit!" Lily spouts, then lowers her voice. "Holy shit, you are?"

"Yes, and I'm sorry I didn't tell you. I didn't tell anyone, I didn't even disclose it on my hiring materials."

"You lied to HR? That's iconic," Lily leans closer. She doesn't look mad, just surprised, and maybe even excited. "And holy shit, your *scent matches?*"

"I know. I'm sorry that I didn't—"

"Who helps you through your heat? You've never taken days off, when do you—" Alice gasps and her eyes widen. "The week you were all 'sick'?"

Alice folds her hands in her lap and nods. She's just going to have to let Lily mentally work through this one before they can move on to anything else.

"No wonder they've been staring at you... They want you to have their *babies!*"

"Something like that."

"This is the biggest news I've heard all year, maybe in my whole life," Lily says. "Why don't you look happy about this? They're perfect. Aren't you thrilled? I've never met anyone with a scent match!"

Thrilled.

Alice has not been thrilled for a moment that she has scent matches. She has admitted to herself, though, that being with them is indeed thrilling. Electrifying, even.

"It is very complicated right now," Alice says. Lily's brows furrow, equal parts concern and confusion. "By no fault of theirs, though. You're right, they're perfect. They do want me to have their babies, definitely. It's, um. . . I'm the problem."

Lily puts a warm hand on her friend's arm. She's wonderful, and Alice is filled with so much love for her in this moment. Of all of the companies in the city, they ended up as interns at the same time in the same place, and even though Alice has been keeping a huge secret from her for years, Lily is immediately open and kind, and offering comfort and friendship when she could be closed off and hurt.

"I think that for a long time, I haven't felt like I can bet on myself," Alice says. "I couldn't imagine that they were betting on anything other than the scent match."

Lily doesn't rush to tell her this isn't true, or that Alice should believe in herself more; she just waits and listens.

"Have you ever thought about leaving Labyrinth?" Alice asks. Lily blinks at the apparent subject shift, then looks around to make sure none of their coworkers are in the food court near them.

"Constantly," Lily admits. "I have a couple of freelance clients I help out, and I know I could get more, but I'm scared to make the jump, you know?"

"Mhm." Alice takes a long gulp of water.

Lily is one of the most talented designers on staff; a dream to collaborate with, a sharp designer, great at taking feedback, and more thorough than any of the other designers on the team. There's a reason Lily's request box is always full. "What would you think about starting a boutique agency with me?"

After a moment of shocked silence, a grin spreads across Lily's face. "Tell me more."

* * *

Things move quickly when you've finally found a direction. Alice put in her two weeks notice just ten days after first talking with Lily about starting their own agency. Logan about shit a brick when she told him, his entire face flushed a pale white. He begged, was angry, tried to guilt her, and then finally landed on an unhappy acceptance.

She will officially accept clients come the new year, and will have the last few weeks of December to set up the rest of their paperwork and accounts. All the money she'd been stowing away for the last two years was enough to get them started and for her to live on without income for the next few months, at least.

She and Lily put together a website and some simple ads and already they had four people on their waitlist for January. They would be small accounts, but accounts nonetheless, and the thought was electrifying.

Caleb and Grant are still giving her space, but when Logan announces to the whole department that Alice will be leaving them before the new year, they both look up in alarm, Caleb even stands up from his desk.

Alice pulls her shoulders back as she stands next to Logan, unable to keep the slight smile from tugging at her lips.

"And of course we will all miss her very much, so whoever convinces her to stay gets lunch on me for a week. A month," Logan says, attempting to sound like he's joking. Everyone goes back to their own work, though Alice takes a moment to look at both Caleb and Grant before inclining her head towards the stairwell.

She goes first, up the sets of stairs to the roof access, her shoes click against the concrete steps. It's only when she gets outside that she realizes she forgot her coat.

The sun is out for once. It heats her cheeks as she closes

her eyes, she dips her head back. It's not long before the door presses open revealing Caleb and Grant both out of breath.

"You quit?" Caleb's eyes are still wide as he speaks, almost yelling. "Is this because of us? We could have talked about it!"

Grant shrugs off his coat and places it around Alice's shoulders, and Caleb, still huffing and puffing and generally in a fit about this, untangles the red scarf and knots it around her neck. The scent of their clothes would be comforting enough to put her right to sleep under different circumstances.

Satisfied with her level of warmth, they stand back and wait for an explanation.

"I'm starting my own agency. With Lily." Their stunned expressions mirror how she's felt about all of this since deciding to take the plunge.

"That's amazing," Grant breathes, but Alice isn't finished.

"I didn't believe that you would choose me because *I* didn't think that I would choose me," Alice admits. "I didn't know exactly what I wanted to do with my life, only what I *didn't* want to do, or was too afraid to do. What I didn't want to be."

"And what is it that you want to do?" Caleb asks.

Alice looks out over the city. The sun sets early this time of year and is already creeping its way down the horizon casting a yellow glow over the skyline.

"I want to see what I can do on my own out there. See if I can make something great."

"You will," Grant says.

"I will, I think," Alice agrees. "I hope."

Despite the late nights spent planning and working

after work, and the perpetual lack of sleep without Caleb and Grant, the tired smile that's been living on her face for the last couple of days remains. "But I don't want to be alone."

Caleb and Grant both freeze, neither of them allowing them to believe she's saying what they're desperate for her to say. A cold wind blows between them, lifting the ends of her hair around her face.

She stands up straighter and looks at them both. The men who have been nothing but good to her, who want nothing more than to love her.

"I need to warn you that I'm a horrible cook," she says. "I leave the bathroom messy most mornings because I snooze my alarm way past when I know I should."

Grant's eyebrows inch towards each other.

"I'm a people pleaser who has a hard time saying no, and to add to that neurotic cocktail, I'm a workaholic."

"You put way too many exclamation points in your emails," Caleb adds.

"It's excessive, really," Alice agrees.

"Not to mention you're exceptionally stubborn," Grant says.

"*So* fucking stubborn," Alice nods. "I can't help myself."

Grant and Caleb both step closer, close enough that any of them could touch if they just reached out. The beast inside her is quiet, not pining and yearning and aching for once. Just a quietness settling in herself.

"I don't want to be alone," she repeats, then emboldened by them not telling her to fuck right off, "I want to do the thing where we try to love each other and keep trying to make things work, even after we learn all the bad things. Especially after."

"You mean it?" Grant asks. His arms are crossed over his

broad chest, like they always are when he's playing hard-ball. "Because if you mean it, you can't mean it halfway. If you say you're in, it's all in, or nothing, baby."

"And if you change your mind?" Alice asks.

"We won't," Caleb says, his voice gruff. "I am so sure about this, Alice."

Alice's pulse races beneath her skin and she grins, taking one of each of their hands in hers. Something wholly and perfectly right clicks into place. She pulls them towards her and they wrap her in their arms. The tightest hug between the three of them as they bask in the quietness of the rooftop, the whole city is at a standstill as the sun sets in the distance.

fourteen

IT'S BEEN three months since Alice quit her job at Labyrinth Solutions. Nothing that Logan said could make her stay, though he did try his best before witnessing Grant and Caleb walk her out of the building with a box of her desk trinkets and mugs in their arms.

Lily officially followed suit a month later, making their new company Walton Marketing her full-time job.

It was humble beginnings, but they were making just enough that both of them could do it full-time. It was enough to live on and, soon, would be enough to hire some more help. Alice worked fifty-hour weeks. Sometimes from the office, they'd set up in the upstairs loft, sometimes from the local library or her favorite cafe.

Even when it's a lot, it's never tedious.

The deadlines are her own and she doesn't have to deal with any of the corporate nonsense that she'd grown accustomed to.

It's hard work, but she's steadily getting new clients. And between her and Lily, they'd need to hire a few more helping hands soon. Before the end of the year, they'd be a team of five if everything went the way she wanted it to.

Tonight she's four-nonstop-hours deep into finishing up a project for a new client when warm hands descend onto her shoulders. She immediately relaxes her hunched posture and pushes off her headphones.

"Five already?" she asks with a yawn. She tilts her head back and accepts a kiss from Grant, still in his work clothes, his tie loose around his neck. "You're handsome."

"Thank you." he kisses her again. "But it's actually six, baby." She curses and looks at her desk clock where, sure enough, it's already six. "You need to eat something."

She motions to the half-eaten sleeve of saltines next to her keyboard, which pulls a laugh out of Grant. He swivels her chair to face him and kisses her some more before pulling her up into a hug. She lets his scent wrap around her, pressing her nose into his chest. Her favorite part of any day.

"We ordered Thai."

"Oh, thank god." Alice squeezes him one last time before patting his butt and leaving him to change while she investigates the Thai situation downstairs.

Caleb is already serving noodles and curry onto plates for the three of them. She holds him around the waist, standing on tiptoes to peer over his shoulder.

"Did you get rangoons?" she whispers and feels a laugh shake his chest.

"Of course." Caleb reaches into the plastic bag and removes one more styrofoam takeout box. Her mouth waters just thinking about it. "How was it today?"

"Great!" Alice starts on getting out forks and cups—the blue ones, her favorites—moving around him in the kitchen. "By some miracle, all the clients we billed this week paid *on time* and Lily delivered a bunch of projects, so things are looking good for next week."

"And how were you feeling?"

"Ah," Alice shrugs. "Maybe just a little antsy."

Her second heat is just about due, they can all tell. She's clingier than usual and can't stop messing with the nest. The blankets have been washed and re-washed and nearly every hoodie owned by Grant and Caleb has been commandeered, either to be worn by Alice around the house or put over pillows like cases. The blackout curtains were secured, the whole house cleaned top to bottom, and she's been having the hot flashes that tell her it really won't be long now.

"Do you feel sick? Feverish?"

"I feel hungry," she says, but doesn't hold his eyes. He always knows when she's keeping something from him, it's obnoxious. "Now stop worrying and feed me a rangoon please."

Caleb rolls his eyes before opening the box and sliding it over.

"Thank you, thank you," she says before promptly burning the inside of her mouth on the filling of a full wonton stuffed in her mouth.

Caleb and Grant sit on either side of her at the bar and she tugs at each of their stools until they inch closer to her. Satisfied, she digs into her food. She's starving and anxious about what she wants to ask them. The solution to both is shoveling food into her mouth while the guys update her on the day's office drama.

Scott isn't nearly as productive as she was, but he's really stepped up in the role. Logan has had to do a lot more of his own work, though.

After ten minutes of her nodding and humming like

she's listening and then asking for them to repeat themselves when they ask a question, Caleb and Grant put their forks down and turn to face her.

"What is it?"

"What is what?" she says around a mouthful of noodles.

"You're acting weird," Caleb says. "Distracted."

"I'm not."

Grant raises an eyebrow, not buying it for a second.

Alice finishes chewing and then drains the rest of her glass of water. She knows she shouldn't be nervous, but she can't help herself. It's not a small thing, what she wants.

"I want to finish the mating bond before I go into heat," she blurts and both of the men's jaws gape open. "With both of you."

"You do?" Grant manages at the same time Caleb says, "You're sure?"

She is sure, as sure as she's ever been about anything—she has been for a while. At Christmas, both Caleb and Grant expressed that they did in fact *want* to bond with her, but not until she was ready. She was thankful for their patience and even more thankful that they hadn't brought it up since.

And well, now she is ready.

"I think it'll help," she says. "My mom says heat is less painful if you're bonded."

"That may be true," Caleb nods.

"But that's not the only reason," Alice says, then releases a huge breath. She looks between them and lets them each pick up a hand. "I love you both. I want to be bonded to you permanently."

"You do?" Caleb's face goes soft.

"How could I not?"

"Great question," Grant says, earning a little smile. "You don't feel rushed, do you?"

"No. I want this. And I want to do it before I'm so consumed by my heat that I can barely remember my own name, much less one of the most important moments of my life."

When neither of them says yes, she goes on by saying, "I know we haven't talked about it in a while, and if anything has changed for either of you—"

"It hasn't," Grant assures. "Couldn't."

"I've wanted this since the first day," Caleb admits. "I've always wanted this to be forever."

"Anything you want," Grant agrees. "We'd wait as long as you need."

The heat is really making her hormones volatile because their assurance makes her eyes well with big, sappy tears. She's turning into her mother.

"Then I want it," Alice says.

"When?" Caleb asks, suddenly sounding very urgent about this.

"I thought maybe. . . tonight?"

Caleb and Grant's eyes meet across Alice for just a minute before they spring into action, Caleb unbuttoning his shirt while Grant deftly plucks Alice up from the stool.

"Wait, now?" She squawks, but clings to Grant with her legs around his waist.

"Baby, we've been waiting for this moment. We're not going to waste another second," Grant says.

"Gotta do it before you change your mind," Caleb chimes in. Alice laughs loudly before pulling herself flush against Grant's strong chest. Over his shoulder, Caleb's already stripped off his shirt and she can see there's a bulge in the front of his pants, ever eager for her.

Grant goes for the nest instead of their bedroom, dropping to his knees and resting her on her back gently atop the pile of pillows and blankets. Caleb clicks on the strings of lights while Grant gets to work kissing up Alice's body and stripping off her clothes.

In her mind, she planned to look a bit sexier for this moment; maybe some lingerie or a silky slip instead of the matching sweat suit she wears to work on days when she has no meetings. Her hair, too, is in two frizzy red braids that whole chunks of hair have escaped from. But the way both men look at her like she's the most radiant thing in the world, she knows she doesn't need any of that to enamor them.

Caleb climbs onto the bed, crawling over her until her lips can fuse with his in a kiss that sears them both. His tongue is hot, probing immediately into her mouth—no grace, there's hardly ever grace with him—he is all heat and excitement and passion, and Alice adores it.

"I love you, I love you," Caleb breathes against her mouth. "Loving you like this is all I can think about sometimes, the way we all fit together."

A little moan escapes Alice when she feels a stubbled chin scrape between her thighs. It takes nothing for her to be soaked this close to going into her heat when it seems that one of them even ghosting their hand across her back will make her flood with slick.

"Baby," Grant whines, as if the sight of her wet and spread before him is painful to him.

"Get me ready for you," she says. Something devilish and possessive draws across his face and he gets to work, licking and nipping and teasing her.

"We're going to need a couple of orgasms from you,

Sweetheart, can you do that for us?" Caleb asks, watching Grant with rapt interest.

Alice is not often as patient as they'd like. They'd prefer she have a minimum of three orgasms before demanding their knots. They say she's bossy and impatient, not a glimpse of people-pleasing tendencies when it comes to being pleasured.

"You sit back and let us have two, then we'll give you what you want, you greedy girl." Caleb twists at one of her nipples, the sting overwhelming her senses as Grant presses his tongue into her hole again and again.

Two orgasms might not be difficult, not when she's already so close to her first.

She twists her fingers in Grant's hair, pulling him closer to her and grinding against his tongue which he swirls around her clit. When Grant sucks it into his mouth, he adds three fingers into her, sliding effortlessly inside.

"Caleb," Grant groans, and pulls his head away from Alice so Caleb can take a turn lapping at her pussy while Grant keeps his relentless fingering, pressing circles to her g-spot. Grant holds Caleb's head to Alice, his grip tight on the back of Caleb's neck.

"She tastes perfect, doesn't she?" Grant asks. Caleb can only moan his ascent. "That's our mate, baby. That taste was made for us."

Alice groans, her hands seeking purchase anywhere and finding Caleb's forearm.

As she squeezes his arm tighter, he only licks faster.

"That's it," Grant coos. "He's doing you just right, isn't he, Alice?"

"Yes," she breathes, and then repeats herself, chanting *yes, yes, yes* as Grant's fingers and Caleb's mouth bring her right over the edge, drenching Grant's palm with more of her slick that Caleb licks off of his fingers.

Alice tries to catch her breath, but before she can, Grant is already rubbing slick from her slit down to her tight hole. His thumb rubs circles around the entrance and her breath hitches every time he presses.

"One more, baby. Can you give us another before we fuck you?" Grant asks. He sounds so sweet, not like the demanding pleasure devil he really is.

"Okay." She whines and writhes beneath Grant's fingers. "But hurry."

Grant and Caleb laugh, then communicate something in their silent way before Grant removes himself between her legs and lies down beside her.

"Come here, baby," Grant says, and tugs her until her front is pressed to his chest, his rigid cock squeezed between them. She wants to touch it and suck it into her mouth until he loses himself in her, but she knows he won't allow it. They have different plans for her tonight.

"There you are," Grant says, his face now level with hers. She tastes herself on his tongue when they kiss and quickly gets lost in it, kissing and breathing him in all while rubbing her body against his, hoping to make him even harder and tempt him into giving her what she really wants.

A hot open mouth laps at her ass before Alice feels something slide into her cunt. She gasps at the smooth, cold intrusion as it slowly pushes her open. It's a toy, one that's thicker than either of them, and Caleb works it in by degrees, one centimeter at a time, then out, before pressing it in a little farther. Her slick makes it glide easily, but she has to breathe deeply through the stretch.

She tries to lift her ass higher in the air, her face resting against Grant's neck as he breathes encouragement into her ear.

"That's a big cock, love, but look at that. You're taking it perfectly."

"I am?" she gasps as it slips in a little farther.

Caleb's hand rubs soothing circles across her ass and lower back. "Just breathe sweet thing, that's right, you're doing so good."

Caleb fucks her with the toy and she expands around it. The stretch is intense but exhilarating, and pain morphs to overwhelming pleasure. She feels dizzy, gripping her mate for dear life as her other rocks the dildo into her. "Do you think you can come around this?"

"I don't—*ah*." Caleb must've hit a button on the dildo because it clicks to life, vibrating inside her and shaking her entire cunt. It moves, too, she can feel it thrusting inside of her, eliciting the most inhuman noises from her mouth.

"How'd we get such a perfect Omega?" Caleb asks.

She moans again, long and loud in Grant's ear, and feels his dick twitch against her stomach.

"That's right, keep feeling that." Grant licks up her neck, tasting the salt and sweat there. Alice thinks he might complete their mating bond right then, but instead, he peppers kisses over her.

Her pussy pulses around the shaking toy that thrusts into her G-spot and she's caught off guard by the orgasm that sweeps over her. A cold sweat covers her skin as she comes, and comes, around the toy, tightening around it as if trying to push it out of herself or suck it in farther, she's not sure.

"Good, good girl coming for us like that," Grant mutters in her ear. "Our perfect girl."

"Alpha," she pleads, and maybe it's the desperation in

her voice, but they don't make her wait. Caleb pulls the toy from her slick hole and Grant readjusts her so that she's higher on his body and his cock is lined up right at her entrance.

There's no preamble before Grant is sliding home in her. He's less thick than the toy was, but warmer and she is so addicted to the feel of their cocks inside of her that it feels like a slice of heaven.

Alice looks over her shoulder for Caleb, who is rubbing something on his cock, watching intently as his mates join together.

"You'll...be in my," Alice breaks on a moan as Grant pushes faster into her cunt. "In my ass?"

"No, sweetheart," Caleb says. "Not quite."

Alice's face twists in confusion, but Grant's knot almost breaching her entrance makes her breath hitch.

Caleb inches between their legs and rubs his slick head between her ass cheeks and down to where Grant fucks her from below.

Alice understands all at once what they plan to do: *both of them inside her.*

She groans at the thought and gasps as Caleb slips two fingers in alongside Grant's cock.

"It won't fit," she breathes. "There's no way you both can fit."

"We will," Grant says. "We've got you, baby."

Grant steadies his thrusting to a stop and all three of them hold their breath as Caleb lines himself up. With excruciating slowness, he presses his cock against Grant's in her hole, stretching her wider than the toy, wider than either of their knots, filling her until she feels she might faint at the sensation.

"Breathe, sweetheart," Caleb says and she and Grant

both take labored breaths. As she relaxes, Caleb can slip in farther, and after a pause, he begins to thrust. "That's unreal. It's. . . *fuck.*"

Grant and Alice both moan, while Grant's mouth is on her neck again, sucking and nipping and licking.

"Do it," Alice whispers, "Please, Alpha."

Grant's hips pulse, pumping just once deeper into her as his teeth bite down on the soft part of her shoulder, completing the mating bond in one glorious moment, connecting them indelibly forever. By the way his hips jerk, Alice knows he's coming in her as he does, and through the bond she can feel his extreme pleasure, only heightening her own.

She feels more than that, though. There's his tenderness and love, the protectiveness he feels, and devotion to both her and Caleb, it's all there in the bond, and he can feel all of her just the same.

Unlatching, he licks at her neck, sealing the wound that already tingles as it heals to a light scar. They breathe together, hearts thundering against each other, and kiss until Alice is dizzy and her chin is bright red from his stubble.

When they pull apart, Alice turns again to study Caleb whose face is screwed up in concentration, like he's trying his hardest not to go into a rut.

"Pull out, angel," Grant tells him, and Caleb does. Grant follows suit, and turns Alice around so she is laying her back on his front, just like the first night he brought her here when she had been so sure the three of them couldn't be together.

Caleb wastes no time crawling over her and mounting her again, sliding to the hilt of his knot and falling immediately into a feverish rut.

Alice tugs his head down to her other shoulder and as his knot presses into her, she bursts, coming around his cock as his teeth sink into her skin—marking her as his forever and sealing their bond while his semen mixes with Grant's inside of her.

She's pumped full and feeling her own emotions alongside Grant's, and Caleb's, mingling together as perfectly as their scents do. It's the most perfect blend of the three of them, now bonded for life, mated to one another.

"I love you," Grant says as Caleb licks at his bite. "I love you, I love you, I love you."

Alice reaches up and holds his head. They're all sweaty messes, but together like this, finally bonded, they're perfect.

Whole.

Completely and joyfully matched.

epilogue

From: Alice Walton <alice@waltonmarketing.com>
To: Caleb Everett, Grant Jones
Date: Monday, October 6, 2025 at 10:15 AM
Subject: Welcome to Walton

Dear Caleb and Grant,

My name is Alice Walton, and I am excited to welcome you to the Walton Marketing team. As our QA and legal needs grow, I believe you two will make an excellent addition to the team.

If you have any questions about work, please do not ask me when I'm off the clock, as my partners are very intense about leaving work at work—even if work is from our upstairs loft. I am thrilled to now have your expertise on the team and am looking forward to working with you both.

Best,

Alice Walton

____

From: Caleb Everett
To: Alice Walton, Grant Jones
Date: Monday, October 6, 2025 at 10:19 AM
Subject: Re: Welcome to Walton

Alice,

You are the brightest light in my world. Grant's too.

Love,
Caleb

____

From: Grant Jones
To: Alice Walton, Caleb Everett
Date: Monday, October 6, 2025 at 10:24 AM
Subject: Re: Re: Welcome to Walton

Alice,

I second Caleb's sentiments. Thrilled to be on your team.

Yours forever,
Grant

THE END

acknowledgments

Writing a book is a massive task. Publishing that said book is a completely different animal. As much as writing is viewed as a solitary craft (the writer plus their blank word doc, cursor blinking back at them), it is so much more of a collaborative process than the one name on the cover would give it credit for.

First, I want to thank all of my friends who read this book and helped me get it into shape. Thank you to my besties Rebecca, Rachel, Lizzie, and Shayla for reading the first draft, hyping it up, and giving really helpful feedback over long phone calls and voice memos. Rachel, you should put Omegaverse Scholar on your resume, I am so serious.

Thank you to my sister, Jacqueline, who reads everything I write with enthusiasm and love—you exist in every sister relationship I've ever written.

Thank you to Elaine Richards for being a thoughtful and thorough editor (sorry for all the parentheticals, I cannot help myself!)

Thank you to my agent Bethany Weaver for cheering me on and answering many, many questions as I've gone about self-publishing this book.

Thank you to Jenn, Naj, and the team at Qamber for the amazing cover, and Anastasia Kurtuluş for the art. I am so beyond obsessed with how you brought the concept to life!

Thank you to my husband. I adore you. Nothing begrudging about it.

Finally, thank you to anyone who read this book. I write because I love it, and I share my writing because I hope someone else might love it, too. Though this is my first book, it will not be my last.

about the author

Naomi Phillips is a writer of sweet and spicy romances. She lives in Utah with her husband and their cat, whom they adore. This is her debut novel.

Find her online for updates on her next releases:
Instagram: @naomiphillips_writes
X: @writer_naomi

www.ingramcontent.com/pod-product-compliance
Lightning Source LLC
Chambersburg PA
CBHW061544310726

48972CB00008B/2609